Patrick Chamoiseau

Solibo Magnificent

Patrick Chamoiseau's other books include *Tex-aco,* which won France's Prix Goncourt, and *Creole Folktales.* He lives in Martinique.

D0004012

VINTAGE

INTERNATIONAL

Also by **Patrick Chamoiseau**

Creole Folktales

Texaco

Acclaim for **Patrick Chamoiseau's**

Solibo Magnificent

"[A] beautifully written novel."   —*The Wall Street Journal*

"Chamoiseau's prose, as always, offers heady delights."
—*The Miami Herald*

"A brilliant novel."   —*Financial Times*

"Chamoiseau keeps . . . perfect pitch operating throughout."   —*The Village Voice*

"Steeped in the vibrant color and lush vegetation, in the hot
spices and oppressive sun of the tropics, the prose bristles
with sensual energy."   —*St. Petersburg Times*

"At once funny and elegiac, this novel delivers Chamoiseau's return gift to his island's storytellers and confirms his
place among them."   —*Publishers Weekly*

"*Solibo Magnificent* . . . is both meaty and a cry on behalf of a
drowning culture."   —*Newsday*

"As long as story tellers as gifted as Chamoiseau share their
words, audiences will have reason to celebrate."
—*The Columbus Dispatch*

"A wonderful novel."   —*Kirkus Reviews*

Solibo Magnificent

Patrick Chamoiseau

Translated from the French and Creole by
Rose-Myriam Réjouis and Val Vinokurov

Afterword by

Rose-Myriam Réjouis

Vintage International

Vintage Books

A Division of Random House, Inc.

New York

FIRST VINTAGE INTERNATIONAL EDITION, APRIL 1999

Translation copyright © 1997 by Rose-Myriam Réjouis and Val Vinokurov
Afterword copyright © 1997 by Rose-Myriam Réjouis

All rights reserved under International and Pan-American Copyright
Conventions. Published in the United States by Vintage Books, a division of
Random House, Inc., New York, and simultaneously in Canada by Random
House of Canada Limited, Toronto. Originally published in France as *Solibo
Magnifique* by Editions Gallimard, Paris, in 1988. Copyright © 1988 by
Editions Gallimard. First published in the United States in hardcover
by Pantheon Books, a division of Random House, Inc., New York, in 1998.

Vintage Books, Vintage International, and colophon are trademarks
of Random House, Inc.

The Library of Congress has cataloged the Pantheon edition as follows:
Chamoiseau, Patrick
[Solibo Magnifique. English]
Solibo Magnificent / Patrick Chamoiseau ; translated from the French and
Creole by Rose-Myriam Réjouis and Val Vinokurov.
p. cm.
ISBN 0-679-43236-1
I. Réjouis, Rose-Myriam.   II. Vinokurov, Val.   III. Title.
PQ3949.3.C45S6514   1998
843—dc21   97-18185

Vintage ISBN: 0-679-75176-9

Author photograph © Jacques Sassier/Gallimard

www.randomhouse.com/vintage

Printed in the United States of America
10 9 8 7 6 5

Hector Biancotti,
this word is for you.

P.C.

I am from a country where an oral, traditional, constrained literature is becoming a written literature, untraditional and just as constrained. My language attempts to construct itself at the frontier of the written and the spoken word, attempts to signal such a passage—which is most assuredly very arduous in any literary approach. . . .

I evoke a synthesis, a synthesis of the written syntax and of the spoken rhythm, of writing's "acquiredness" and of the oral "reflex," of the loneliness of writing and of the participation in the communal chant—a synthesis which seems to me interesting to attempt.

EDOUARD GLISSANT

Mé zanmis ôté nouyé!?
[Oh God my friends! Where are you!?]

ALTHIERRY DORIVAL
(Haitian singer)

What is at the center of the narration for me is not the explication of a strange fact but the *order* that this strange fact develops in itself and around itself: the drawing, the symmetry, the network of images which assembles around it, as in the formation of a crystal.

ITALO CALVINO

Contents

After the Word (Document of the Memory)

Bringing the Word

Translators' Note

Translators' footnotes are distinguished from the author's by [brackets]. Generally, we have left Creole dialogue in the original, and, unless the author provides a literal French translation, we footnote our own translations of the Creole. The only exceptions are occasional cases of Creolized French (which we replace with an invented "Creolized" English) and one instance where the author himself footnotes his Frenchified version of a Creole outburst (which we translate literally in brackets in the body of the text, following the original). Unusual words are included in the Glossary (such words are asterisked the first time they appear in the text), and the more colorful names are likewise glossed in the back of the book. Rose-Myriam Réjouis's Afterword, "Sublime Tumble," explores the intricate interlinguistic dynamics in Chamoiseau's work.

R.M.R.
V.V.

The ethnographer:

—But, Papa, what to do in such a situation?

—Laugh at it first, *said the tale-teller.*

Before the Word

Document of the Calamity

Incident Report

Visit to the scene by Chief Inspector Evariste Pilon, officer of the Department of Criminal Investigation.

Annum one thousand nine hundred and . . .

The second of February, 06:00 hours:

The undersigned, Evariste Pilon, officer of the Police of Urban Safety of Fort-de-France, Criminal Brigade, officer of the Department of Criminal Investigation;

Standing the night shift;

Informed by Chief Sergeant Philémon Bouaffesse, service number 000.01, that he has just discovered, after the intervention of Madame Lolita *Boidevan,* street merchant residing at Pont-Démosthène by the great canal, the corpse of a man under a tamarind tree in a place known as the Savanna;*

Per Article 74 of the Code of Penal Procedure, at 06:11 hours, notice has been given to His Honor, the District Attorney, who assigns us to the matters specified in this text;

We immediately visit the site,

Where, being in the presence of the Chief Sergeant who has waited for us per our request and has directed us to the location where he has discovered the body;

We note the following:

Under a tree situated 6.5 meters to the left of the memorial, on the border of the path, lies the corpse of a man of about fifty years of age. He is wearing an open white shirt, unbuttoned gray trousers with an unhooked black leather belt in its loops. The feet are bare. A shoe containing a sock rolled up in a ball is at the level of his right hip. The clothes are stained and in disarray. The sleeves of the shirt are raised up to the elbows. The pants are rolled up to the knees.

The body is lying on its back, between the roots of the tree. The arms, spread wide in the form of a cross, are maintained in an elevated position. The right knee is tucked in. The head is inclined toward the left. The legs are oriented toward the memorial.

The corpse is cold, affected by rigor mortis. It shows no sign of putrefaction. No scratch, abrasion, or contusion is seen on the face or hands. The face is grayish, ears purplish, a pink froth is detected around the mouth and nose. The eyes are wide open. No trauma visible on either chest, belly, arms, or legs. The skull bears no apparent injuries.

Upon completion of his examination concomitant to ours, Dr. Gabriel Siromiel submits a written report with his sworn opinion, given in honor and conscience, in which it appears that the death occurred between 04:00 and 05:00 hours and that its cause is as yet unknown.

Around the body are a peasant drum, four small plain glass bottles, empty and open, a potato packing crate, smashed, and miscellaneous debris: crushed tamarinds, leaves which are not from the tamarind tree. The place seems to have been trampled on. No footprints are clearly visible.

Above the skull, between the roots, there is a gray hat with a light-colored ribbon, an unlaced shoe, a sock rolled up in a ball, numerous shards of glass. A strong smell of urine is detected here.

Continuing our examination of the scene, under a root we discover a knife about fifteen centimeters long with a metallic handle, a smashed razor blade; in front of the tree, at about a meter from the body, are a straight line of large stones, some packing crates, an empty demijohn, two empty small bottles, other debris.

We note the presence of an extinguished torch in a knothole.

All statements and useful photographs collected, we extract from pocket of corpse a razor, two ten-franc bills, a fifty-centime coin, a red-checkered cotton handkerchief.

We impound the drum, the small bottles of plain glass, the potato crate, the knife with the metallic handle, the razor blade, the demijohn, all of which we order to be taken immediately, in special packaging, to the interregional police laboratory, for the purposes of content analysis and for the collection and photographic enlargement of fingerprints present on these objects. To this end, we include the fingerprints of the victim, which we collected ourselves, along with the present package for the purpose of comparison.

Once these operations are carried out, we have the body taken to the Clarak Hospital morgue, where, in accordance with the requirements of His Honor the District Attorney, it awaits autopsy to be performed by Dr. Lélonette, physician-specialist presiding at the Court of Appeals of Fort-de-France.

The scene of the crime being out in the open, we cordon off the area around the tree with Vauban barriers and post two guards.

Author of the above report,
duly reviewed and co-signed by Dr. Siromiel
and Chief Sergeant Bouaffesse,

Officer of the Department of Criminal Investigation
E. PILON

Chapter 1

My friends!

Here the Master of the Word

swerves onto the sharp curve of destiny

and plunges us

into ill-luck

(Tears for whom?

For Solibo.)

During a Carnival

evening in Fort-de-France between Fat Sunday and Ash Wednesday, the storyteller Solibo Magnificent died, throat snickt by the word, exclaiming: *Patat' sa!* . . . That potato! . . . His audience, believing they had heard the standard invitation for vocal response, saw it their duty to reply: *Patat' si!* This potato! . . . The harvest of fate that I shall narrate to you happened on a day whose date is unimportant since time signs no calendar here.

But first, dear friends, before I speak of this atrocity, I ask one favor: Imagine only an upright Solibo Magnificent, in his most handsome days. These words are spoken only after the hour of his death—so tragic!—and not even during the due orations of a wake, by his sweet-herb-scented body. Suspecting a crime, the police picked him up as if he were a bit of ordinary garbage, and the coroner autopsied him into little pieces. They cut his head bone open to pick the cream of his brain for the mystery of his death. They cut open his chest, cut out his lungs and heart. They spilled his blood into clear glass tubes, and from his open stomach they impounded his last sharkstew. And when Sidonise sees him again, sewn up as badly as some miserable shift . . . oh-lord! How does one put into words a sadness so great it refuses to bathe a brave woman's eyes? . . . That is why, dear friends, before I speak, I ask this favor: Imagine Solibo in his most handsome days, always in earnest, blood running back and forth, his body planted in life like an acacia in quicksand. For if in life he was an enigma, today it is much worse: he exists (as the Chief Inspector will realize after and beyond his inquiry) only in a mosaic of memories, and his tales, his riddles, his jokes on life and death have all dissolved in minds too often sodden.

In the realm of Fort-de-France, he had become a Master-of-the-unanswerable-Word, not by decree of some folkloric institute (the only place where they still celebrate the oral tradition), but by his taste for the word, for speech without commas. He talked, voilà. At the fishmarket where he knew everyone, he talked at every step, he talked to everyone, to a woman tattling tongue-crazy, available and useless, oh mama! what a gust of blah-blah . . . In the pool hall at the Croix-Mission, at Friday meat market when the beef arrives, in the cathedral courtyard after the devotional, at Louis-Achille Stadium while we screamed at the referee, Solibo talked, he talked ceaselessly, he talked at fairs, talked by the rides, and even more at parties. But he was not some runaway from a psychiatric hospital, one of those loons who jerk out words as casually as they put their feet up. At the Chez Chinotte, oh sanctuary of punch, we gathered to listen to him, and though there wasn't a white hair on his temples and though the tafia* had not yet made his eyes red (only the first dirty yellow had touched the white), a silence welcomed the opening of his mouth: around here it is this that signals and anoints a Master.

For him, I would have wished words his size: inscribed in a simple life and yet higher than life. But around his body the police had scribbled "suspicious death." The police were injustice, humiliation, misapprehension, bringing together the absurdities of power and might, terror and folly. With my soul struck blank, all there is left for me to do is testify, standing here among you, molding my words as in a *Vénéré,* on this lost night of drumming and prayer on which the black souls of Guadeloupe keep vigil till night whitens, remembering the one who died. But look out, friends! When facing these policemen, smile, show your teeth, because, so writes René Ménil,[1] it is by bitter laughter that an era takes revenge on those who are still strutting when the scene is done, and detaches itself from them in anticipation of their actual death.

And so: fatal evening—after the parades, the crowd broke up into the smaller parties (*gragé jounou, touffé-yinyin, zouks* . . .) that Carnival sows in its wake, from Balata field to the hutches of Texaco.* In the downtown air only the cinders of joy survived, and on the isolated hills ka-drums* throbbed syncopations. Under the tamarind trees of the Savanna, that free realm of all that grows, the serbi* enthusiasts had lit dozens of torches and called out their bets while exchanging demijohns of tafia. Other blacks, less unbridled, prayed silently to the holy Madonna of Jossaud about the enigma of a black card among red ones, or the bitchy hesitations of a casino-barrel's ball. Adding the final touch to this setting, the gravel of stars in the sky, the bittersweet breath of the tamarinds, and the cacophony of all kinds of merchants.

His drum on his shoulder, the musician who usually accompanied the words of Solibo Magnificent arrived at the first shadows and set himself up under the oldest of the tamarind trees, by the memorial. He was a nothing of a man, drawn by his bones, his neck whitened with ancient dermatitis, they called him Sucette. This nickname came from his notorious oral attentions to bottles of Neisson rum. With twelve sonorous rat-a-tas and two-three roars of his ka,* Sucette convoked a company under the light of his

---

[1] A Philosopher from around here.

torch. Snap and even faster-than-snap, an audience had gathered, leaving the game tables, avid already for the appearance of Solibo Magnificent: all the words of the old storyteller, rare these days, were good to hear. He gonna come, Sucette? . . . Where is he, huh? You think he gonna come? . . . These impatient ones could never guess that a moment later the police would write down their names in a report, nor even suspect that under certain circumstances and in the name of the Law, simple listeners of krickrack tales turned into *witnesses*.

(List of witnesses extracted from the general report of the preliminary investigation submitted by the Chief Inspector of the precinct:

—Zozor *Alcide-Victor,* retailer, resides at 6 rue François-Arago.

—Eloi *Apollon,* nicknamed Sucette, claims to be drummer of krickrack tales, in reality has no occupation or permanent address.

—*"Bête-Longue"* (inquiries concerning the civil status of this individual are forthcoming), claims to be sailor-fisherman, quite clearly has no occupation, resides in Texaco, near the fountain.

—Lolita *Boidevan,* nicknamed Doudou-Ménar, street vendor of candied fruits, resides at Pont-Démosthène, by the great canal, behind the ravine.

—Patrick *Chamoiseau,* nicknamed Chamzibié, Ti-Cham, or Oiseau de Cham, claims to be "word scratcher," in reality has no occupation, lives at 90 rue François-Arago.

—Richard *Cœurillon,* claims to be a factory worker (?), quite clearly has no occupation, resides at Château-Bœuf on the lower floor.

—Bateau *Français,* nicknamed Congo, manioc grater maker (?), very probably has no occupation, resides in the neighborhood of La-Belfort, Lamentin.

—Charles *Gros-Liberté,* nicknamed Charlo', claims to be musician, in reality has no occupation, resides at rue du 8-Mai, Dillon Estates.

—Justin *Hamanah,* nicknamed Didon, claims to be master jobber at the vegetable market, in reality has no occupation, resides at 10 rue Schœlcher, Terres-Sainville.

—Conchita *Juanez y Rodriguez,* of Colombian nationality, has no occupation, looks like a hooker, has no permanent residence.

—Antoinette Maria-Jésus *Sidonise,* sherbet vendor, resides at rue des Abymes, Trenelle.

—Pierre Philomène *Soleil,* nicknamed Pipi, claims to be a jobber, in reality has no occupation, resides at Rive-Droite-Levassor.

—Sosthène *Versailles,* nicknamed Ti-Cal, municipal employee, resides on the new extension of rue Liberté, Volga Plage, known as Independentist.

—Edouard *Zaboca,* nicknamed La Fièvre, claims to be an agricultural worker, in reality has no occupation, resides at Gondeau, Lamentin.

These witnesses have been depositioned by the Chief Sergeant, Philémon Bouaffesse, then by myself, Evariste Pilon. Their statements, and the deplorable incidents that have accompanied them, are the subjects of the written reports enclosed herein.)

Ah! Solibo Magnificent came in at the end of a pirouette. Bushy mustache, straw-broom goatee at the tip of his chin, he had the tafia expert's red-yellow eyes. His white nylon shirt bore gold cufflinks, yes, and silver sleeve-tighteners. His pants, worn to death, fell neatly on his varnished boots: ah, Solibo had really earned his name's other half! . . . He lifted his little hat to greet the audience: Ladies and gentlemen if I say good evening it's because it isn't day and if I don't say good night it's the cause of which the night will be white tonight like a scrawny pig on his bad day at the market and even whiter than a sunless béké* under his take-a-stroll umbrella in the middle of a canefield *é krii?** . . . [1]

—*E kraa!** the company had replied.

So joe, while far away the murmur died, exhausted, the Master of the Word spoke, spoke inoculating into his audience an incurable fever. It was not about understanding what was said, but about being open to it, letting it carry you away, because Solibo would become a throaty sound fluttering higher than the song of a solitary clarinet when Stélio the musician breathed into it.

All night, the vocal chords had thundered. Eager to prove they were paying attention to the Master of the Word, the listeners had replied *E kraa!* forcefully. *Misticraa!'s** would ring out like the brass section of a Latin orchestra.

---

[1] See "After the Word" for a tentative restitution of Solibo's words that fatal night.

And when at last the sky paled and a foggy wind announced the dawn, that's when Solibo Magnificent hiccuped on a turn-of-phrase. And without any reason, ladies and gentlemen, he exclaimed: *Patat' sa!* . . . (However, *patat' sa* does not exist in krickrack. The storyteller says *E krii,* asks *Misticrii,** probes to find out *Can someone tell me if all's abed here?* . . . demands his tafia, a drumbeat measured to his speech, but never calls *Patat' sa!* . . .) Yet at that cry of pain, everyone had replied *Patat' si!,* showing that herds of sheep don't always hold the choicest fools.

Snickt like that, he had slipped between the tree roots. His widening gaze seemed to follow the flight of the tale. A hand at his throat, the other over his face, he became as startled as an old man lucky for the first time, while sweat ran off him. Now, thinking back, I've no doubt that the tamarind leaves had moaned, and that they had alerted us by brushing three times against Sucette's torch. And yet, happy as chiggers dug into a dirty foot, everyone waited, especially since demijohns of tafia would oblige the least thirst and the drum man, keeping up what he thought to be an improvised mime of the Master of the Word, unearthed from the drum a cavernous léwoz:* eyes absent, Sucette had left his flesh to fill up the ka, or did the ka bulge in his gut? A vibration melted the man with the barrel, and Sucette's body roared loud as a kidskin. His mouth silently chewed the drum's frequencies. His heel sculpted the sounds. He used the extra hands that drum men keep hidden, and they quickly turned and turned in mountain echoes, crystalline crashes, a rush of life over the earth widening the trails of Carême,* communicating to anyone who could hear (whoever opened himself before it) the expression of a rummy voice, superhuman but familiar: *Yeah! Sucette really had it going on* . . .

Around us, the torches had burned out. In the extinguished Savanna, the Carnival picked through the remains of its joy: the clink of a die, a card rumple, the laughter of a matadora* being kneaded and plowed[1] . . . In the blenching sky, night and day coagulated in a ritual of dew, fog, and icy winds. The demijohns, dry as pumice stones, lay flat near the assembly listening to the drum. The coldness provoked packs of Mélias, Gauloises, and other brands, and the glow of cigarette ends lit the faces. Sometimes, a ka-drum's moan made the large wings of a nose flutter or eyelids shut on the pupils' somber emptiness. The listeners were sitting or crouching on the ground. Some used margarine pots, remains of crates, or rocks as stools. There were women (three, four?), but their faces remained veiled in night because they weren't smoking; the vague gleaming of their Creole earrings indicated their silhouettes. Perhaps Sucette continued his show by drawing energy from his fatigue. At his side, between the tortuous roots, Solibo lay dead. His nylon shirt had turned yellow with sweat and molded to his dry body, one of the gold cufflinks had yielded, freeing the sleeve in folds up to the elbow. The legs of the pants were raised too, as if in anticipation of December rain. We discerned the hair on his thin legs (curled like pepper seeds), the accordion of his socks, the dazzle (oh la la!) of the varnished boots. The tamarinds fell sometimes, but the sound of the drum strangled their tak-tak. And likewise, the wind licked the leaves without our being able to hear it. The bats, flying blackmen, went back to the tree, disappearing into the leaves, reviving the thick odor of tamarinds which had receded at the approach of day. There were no more echoes

---

[1] Doing it standing up.

of the Carnival. Fort-de-France in the distance had taken its sleep, nothing would move until the sun's advent for even though Sucette kept sounding the ka-drum, Solibo didn't stir, not one bit, no.

That scene lasted forever—and could have gone on and on: a tafia-soused audience, sitting in a circle at the crack of dawn, does not inscribe itself in the ephemeral. But then, after eons (exactly three hours, thirty-eight minutes, and twenty-two seconds, says the coroner), a basaltic old man left the assembly and made toward Solibo. His name was Congo and he seemed to owe Death four centuries. Stooping over the body, he had lifted his bakoua* hat and was scratching the white wool of his skull. Head forward, knees bent, butt stuck out, a hand on the small of his back, he seemed kneaded by the caution of these agonizing old blackmen,[1] still afraid of the shades of bad luck. Just when we no longer expected it, Congo straightened up bewildered: *Iye fout! hanman halansé tÿou hot la hou hay dégawé mèdsin, mi Ohibo la ha hay an honjesion anlê noula!* . . . — What now? What are you saying?—Oh, Congo is raving, he pretends that Solibo's dying, that he needs a doctor . . . When the old man managed to make himself understood, the company was electrified. Sucette jumped from his instrument toward the body of the Master. Others, unidentifiable in the confusion and the dark, came nearer, hustling:

---

[1][Translators' note: Chamoiseau uses the French word *nègre* (Negro) in the Creole sense of "man," as in *nèg blanc,* which means "white man." This is why we invent "blackman" to translate a word which is specific to the Creole lexicon, albeit not unrelated to the genealogy of "(my) nigger" as used in contemporary African American speech. Another instance (below) of this Chamoiseau-esque French-Creole slippage occurs in his usage of the Creole slang for homosexual, *maḳoumè* (rendered by us as "auntie"), which the author often spells as *ma commère,* an archaic French appellation for "godmother" or "(a) gossip."]

Hey what what what's happening to him? . . . Sucette roared, provoking in the women the squalling emotion which generally heralds death's descents. Solibo! Solibo get up now! yelled Sucette, Solibo-oh! . . . The straw bundle of the torch burned out, and we lit some debris whose sporadic gleams agitated the shadows. Everything seemed in keeping with a Césairean disaster, astonishment and pain awoke the Savanna. Crabs, rats, long-ones[1] fought each other for the shelter of holes. Thinking themselves under attack, the bats crashed against the predawn sky. Solibo's listeners thronged about him, trampling the roots, shoulders rising behind shoulders, advising remedies which everyone around here brings back from their struggles with death. Cited were: quinine which lights up the extinguished, aloe or Jack's tobacco sap, infusion of Job's seeds, English absinthe, annatto juice which whips up the blood. We invoked a dose of the yellow ash tree, honey-smoked green plantain, Trinidad's weeping blackstone, and, to show how desperate the situation seemed, the Imperial Herb-for-all-ills mixed with powdered cat's claw (sovereign and terrible).

Those who could touch the body couldn't make anything out from this noisy kitchen first aid. They attempted to sit Solibo between the roots, but rigor mortis (which they confused with the Master's resistance) prevented them. So they unbuttoned his shirt while some fanned him with his hat. They slapped him, then they loosened his belt, hoping for a breath. They took off his shoes, rubbed his ears. One, reenacting a scene in a detective movie, blew into his mouth. Another tickled him. Yet another hammered his chest at the

---

[1][The Frenchified Creole *bête-longue* in the original (literally, "long-animal" or "long-beast"), rendered here as "long-one," means snake, and is used in order to avoid pronouncing that dread word.]

site of the heart, as it had been practiced on his wife during a difficult delivery. As they perceived Solibo's progressive stiffness, the cold of his flesh, his eyes' curious fixity, they slackened their care, doubted the efforts of their hands. The reality of the situation imposed itself on some even before being clearly formulated: they ran away, in silent fright, forsaking our witnesses-to-be, fourteen persons, among them three ladies, all certainly imbeciles since it's well known that with a dead body the Law gets involved, and that then, oh boy, your life becomes a high-waist quadrille (the one where you dos-à-dos when the man says to).

The tumult has settled. A rustling of leaves peoples the silence. The tamarinds that let go crash on the moth-eaten grass tak-tak. His back against the trunk, Sucette looks like an empty bag, his arms hang like coolie* hair and his face has less sense in it than a rock in a river. Congo, that immortal tree, sits on a crate, impassive but probably shaken to see Death, his longtime creditor, roam. Tak-tak from time to time, climbing to the sky like a thief, the tree shudders and keeps silent. The ghostly white of the memorial disturbs the little grove's inky leaves. There, to the left, past the edge of the Savanna park, the town reappears under the public lighting: an avenue which runs along a vertigo of stars and scintillation of water, of the sea. Doudou-Ménar (a big woman, who sells candied fruits) whispers psstpsst in the ears of a superb creature, Conchita Juanez y Rodriguez. Stupefied, Antoinette Maria-Jésus Sidonise holds her sherbet maker at arm's length, her eyes are alarmed by an internal distress and she flutters her eyelids as if trying to calm them. She's a small woman, with the flesh and the curves of her forty years atop a child's fragility and finesse. She looks at Solibo like someone who gets vertigo standing at the edge of a crevasse, and every once in a while shakes her head fu-

riously, like a cat shaking off the stale water of a nightmare.
The others say nothing, sculpted around her in shock.

—You'd think that he's dead, frets a red chabin.*
—Nooo! people don't die like this . . .
—And how do they die, hah?
—Not like a soft fruit falling . . .
—*Ha lan-ô yé?* (What is death?—Here, it's Congo
speaking. He has to repeat his question four times because
his way of using the tongue is near extinction around here.)
—We don't know! But, in any case, you don't eat of
the earth and die swollen the same day. If Solibo is dead, it's
been brewing for a while, long before this . . .
—Solibo is dead, then? (Now it's Sucette who worries.)
—If his Carnival rum ran into his baptism cocoa, that
could have made him only dizzy . . . how to know?
—I'll get a medical man! . . . (Here, it's Doudou-
Ménar who breaks off to search for a doctor.)
—A doctor? Ah yes, a doctor could wake him up! . . .
(Sucette approves here.) Go get him, sister!
—*Ha lan-ô yé?*
—Peace, Congo! Solibo isn't dead because that's not
how you die (Sidonise refuses).
—And how do you die, huh?
(Et cetera . . .)

While Doudou-Ménar went away, the discussion (in a
low and respectful tone) circled round and round—like a
conga without maracas—about the modalities of a suitable
death. We touched upon the infinities of thought and upon
fundamental questions. Congo profited from the silences to
slide in with his accent of original African: *Ha lan-ô yé?*
ha lan-ô yé? . . . , a question to which no one paid jack
but which certainly served as a launch pad for vertiginous

thoughts. At the end of a lengthy silence, Congo came back to Solibo's body and, in a congestion of wrinkles, established the diagnosis used as the opening for these words: *Méhié é hanm, Ohibo tjoutÿoute anba an hojèt pahol-la!* . . . Which, translated, may mean: Ladies and gentlemen, Solibo Magnificent is dead, snickt by the word . . .

The old man's confidence discouraged retorts. The company raised a stonework of silence before the truth thus formulated. The only resource, henceforth: to wait for the doctor that Doudou-Ménar had gone to fetch and sustain Solibo with our immobile sadness. We were like dinghies wrecked on a reef: the river of life moved on without us. We looked at each other from within, in a kind of fixed journey through ourselves. *Ho, Solibo's eyes!* . . . Sidonise had slowly pulled down their flown-away eyelids, first with the tips of her fingers, then with her palms, finally with thumbs moistened with tears, but Solibo kept that look which sees the world in other dimensions. To see him here like this, a bundle of dirty laundry in a tuft of roots—it killed us: where is the unshot Kodak photo of his vertical life, of the time his word enveloped the dead at wakes, throwing the funerary nights' anguish to the ground? He would captivate the company with the rhythm of his gestures, no longer spinning the word in the vanishing scene of a traditional wake, but back in the mountain refuge of the blackmen of yesteryear, the new maroons, the lost blackmen, the abandoned ones, the bad apples on the brink of outlawry. These days, he would come under the Savanna's tamarind trees only with Carnival and even then irregularly. Only as the mood would dictate, Sucette would slip the voice of his ka-drum under the Master's word . . . ho, always such class in his gestures and his body, the elegance of a filao pine under a light wind. I had known him during my visits to the market when I had a work on the life of the jobbers in mind. With patience, I got them to accept my notebooks, my pencils, my little tape recorder with batteries that never worked, my unhealthy appetite for tales, all tales, even the most trivial ones. To blend in, I did a few favors here and there, carting off filth, cleaning vegetables, searching for five-centime coins indispensable to the ritual of haggling over prices. My search advanced even more slowly as I had frequent asthma attacks and because I kept forgetting my own work schedule. I wandered then between the stalls, the barrows of the jobbers, and the fruits of the season, in trash among junk, worn haggard by my persistent writing and obscure note-taking. The whole market knew me, from the lowly mango saleswoman to the somber queens—severe and silent—who displayed their magical infusions and their herbs-of-power; all knew me so well that the talk no longer died out at my approach and eventually no one, instead of hello, would ask me: So Ti-Cham, what's the use of writing? . . . Once a pretend-ethnographer, now I dispensed with all distance, living through the torpor of the warm hours by collapsing in the barrows of the jobbers, or by stiffening myself, standing or sitting, as the moment would take me, like old women vendors waiting for the return of a fresh wind. During the market's most feverish hours—noontime and Saturday mornings—I would yell, gesticulate like everybody else, wielding my Creole and my big gestures, busying myself with unfathomable emergencies, no longer caring to listen, to scrutinize or understand life around here, or even, what a shame, the things I would scribble to cheat my remorse. Though I tried during lucid moments to picture myself as a *participant observer,* like the doubtful Malinowski, Morgan, Radcliffe-Brown, or Favret-Saada with his Norman sorcerers, I knew that not one of them had seen himself dissolve thus in what he wanted oh so rigorously to describe. In this market, I was but a kind of parasite, swimming in sterile bliss, whose notes were more like (and still *are,* since I still don't understand jack) the miraculous weapons of the surrealist enchanters.

Who knows what would have become of me if Solibo Magnificent's personality had not awakened my old curiosity, thus allowing me (through him) again to find sense in writing, though I was still unable to repair this bitch of a tape recorder which since my arrival was interested only in its own bronchitic gasps. One morning, Solibo addressed me with the exhausted instead-of-hello question: Chamzibié-ho? what's the use of writing? . . . , then he chatted with me about everything and nothing, the word and the rest, without taking another breath he told me of the origin of the market, seventeen undecipherable tales, gave me news (unasked for) of the senile merchants' financial health, then he spoke to me of charcoal, of yams, of love, of forgotten songs and memory, of memory. This verbal energy seduced me even then. Especially since Solibo used the four facets of our diglossia: the Creole basilect and acrolect, the French basilect and acrolect, quivering, vibrating, rooted in an interlectal space that I thought to be our most exact sociolinguistic reality. I didn't leave him again during that season when he was still seen among the butchers' stalls, jotting down what he said, studying his silences, always dumbfounded by his peculiar audience: an arcanum of indifference and attention, part of the market slowed down to listen—antique Syrians* left their shop windows, and some immortal old women would nod approvingly with his every syllable—while the other part heard nothing. The excitement possessed me. I accumulated notes upon notes and spent feverish nights putting them in order, with the premonitory rage of one wrestling with time: storytellers were rare, I had found one.

But one day Solibo disappeared from the market, disappeared from sight without anyone worrying about the absence of his voice: the market was but noise! . . . Such-and-such had seen him, in this corner, at this or that hour . . . I gave up my cool pursuit, repossessed by my asthma, my jobbers, my trance. And now to find him again here, between the roots, his beautiful fresh-earth color ashen with malediction, could I do anything but stand there numb in the company of others? . . . Among the leaves, the no doubt obituary blackbirds chased the night out of their feathers. Everything was light gray like a cemetery wall, and we, each of us, began to realize the others' presence: Sucette, exhausted and absent, hung to his ka-drum as if it were his mother's underskirt, so much you'd think he was sailing on the other side with Solibo; Zozor Alcide-Victor, the Syrian bastard, a ladies' man and a great dancer, half closed his eyelids below his marijuana cloud and seemed to float among the higher things of life; Pipi, Didon, master jobbers at the vegetable market; Gros-Liberté, a sax player cut adrift since his orchestra had sunk, settled his frustration, mouth wide open, with a bottle of rum; Ti-Cal, a chauffeur for the city hall and a Martinican Progressive Party militant, had leaned his head on his knees and seemed to be working up a nap; Sidonise, the sherbet vendor, and Conchita, the Colombian, standing a little bit apart, torn between the desire to see the end or to go home; Congo, Zaboca, Bête-Longue, and Cœurillon, side by side, eyes bulging, mouth open; and I, stuck at the impossible crossroads of putting myself in parentheses or not. In the distance, the silhouettes of some road sweepers tried to come to life, but we, bathed in a creamy light, waited for Doudou-Ménar, more fixed and opaque than Faulkner's Negroes.

True to her nature, Doudou-Ménar really took off. To go faster, she tucked her basket of grapefruit under one arm and held down her screwpine hat, her immense straw hat, with the other. Her big breasts jumped up and down, but the fat woman ignored them (never burdensome for a chest, these things cannot fall, no). She ran-ran not knowing too much where to, Solibo was he dead or not? and what if he were only drunk, like, say, the Mexican in that stupid western? who's going to find a doctor in Fort-de-France when the sun hasn't even showed up yet? . . . but in her race she drew upon the strength her long day had not been able to exhaust: getting up at sunrise to scald the grapefruit, sweep the house before waking up her son Gustave (a ne'er-do-well, my dear, who wears Pierre Cardin clothes and sings in Spanish in a band where other ne'er-do-wells pretend to be Latins), and sell candied fruit through the favor of the festivities, a way of dealing blows to her debts with the hard swing of a full purse. Her man, Gustave's father, had vanished from the midst of life's traffic, slumped in a festive stupor from which he emerged only after the Carnival, but with empty balls and the muscle all mushy. On the Savanna, Doudou-Ménar very early on had faced severe competition from cake, docoune,* sherbet, and even kilibibi* vendors . . . A whole day going up and down, elbowing through a crowd of spectators tossed about by the monkey business of masquerading blacks. By the end of the afternoon her basket was still half full and the blessed rosary in her purse protected fewer coins than hoped for. Her varicose veins, on the other hand, had swollen. During the final fits of Carnival, she must have adopted the Dominican turtle's gait, stopping at every tree and street corner, and appealed to people playing games beneath torches in the night, to that whole sleepwalking fauna which surrounded the shadows of the tamarind trees. It was after a bout of fatigue that the Fat One, slumped against a root, would hear Sucette's drum, the Magnificent's words, and would rush like all of us into the shelter of his voice. And now, to save Solibo, she hurried in the middle of the night, in a mad dash whose path was only found through this (now regrettable) knowledge: the police station, alas, unlike doctors, Chez Chinotte, or the Syrian shops, never closes its dangerous doors.

That's why, from his desk, the guardian of the peace Justin Philibon, who was sheltering his sleep beneath the logbook, saw Doudou-Ménar flying toward him: Law! call a doctor, there's Solibo fighting an evil spell in the Savanna . . . you hear me, Law? . . . Strengthened by his six years of experience, by his certificate of technical capacity, his Open Sesame into and up the promotion ladder to the rank of sergeant, Justin Philibon placed the index finger of his left hand on the counter, and darted at Doudou-Ménar the look he thought to be justice. Like all the shifts of the Carnival, his had been a feverish one: seven rum-drunks picked up by the patrol, three rastas whose charges were still being drawn up, a senile old man looking for some boat called *Colombia*, a quimboiseur* who was caught desecrating a tomb, and then, of course, the inexhaustible influx of victims with their tales of dirty looks, of fights at the serbi game, of girlfriends whose love forever inspired violence . . . With only his mask of imperial justice and his official manner of unscrewing a Waterman fountain pen over the logbook, Justin Philibon knew how to calm these freaks. But there, in front of Doudou-Ménar vociferating: I tell you that Solibo is fighting an evil spell and you stand in front of me like a moth struck blind by light! You hear me, Law? . . . , he's got nerves as hard as a drumskin. Madame, I am a guardian of the peace, the law it's another matter, it's made in France, you understand? Therefore, calm yourself first and furnish me your full legal name, permanent address, and occupation . . . Finally, tell me what got you so jumpy . . . Saying this, he fixed a stare on Doudou-Ménar, folded back the cover of the logbook, licked an index finger, turned a page then another to the rhythm of his greasy French. Because, he embroidered, it's not like that, ma'am, you are here at a police station and not at the fishmarket, there's officiality, there's regulations, there's the Penal Code and a bunch of stuff like that, you do understand do you not, please? . . . —Solibo is dying, I tell you! the Enormous One spat out, lifting her eyes to heaven, insensitive to procedural refinements. So Justin Philibon suddenly swelled up: You came to bring the circus here, didn't you? . . . At that instant, in the police station which had seemed abandoned, doors opened, the hall filled with light and dark blue silhouettes, a jangling of keys and handcuffs. Silent slow men lined up behind the counter and staked out Justin Philibon, others discreetly obstructed the exit and marked Doudou-Ménar as if she were a soccer forward. The big woman noticed the maneuver, but instead of sanely freaking out, she seemed to take a strange pleasure in it. In this woman, street champion, any threat, any gurgle in the stomach, launched a desire to massacre. She was already regarding the policemen with eyes clotted with hatred. Fearless, her round belly hard, legs apart twisting her purple shoes, arms brought back on the hips like bats' wings, she shone like a tree stripped of its bark.

The lawmen are clawed by this audacity. Justin Philibon closes his Waterman pen with an alarming slowness.

Those who were crowding behind the counter come out, still silent. The sentinels at the door free the rubber pegs, the iron double doors rattle. Two or three put down their helmets, caps, watches on the counter. Others take off Raybans. Some, like thugs, unbutton their shirts not to risk losing a button, and tug their pants. The circle tightens around Doudou-Ménar, who now resembles a mad dog. A primitive shadow darkens all eyes. While a furious silence makes the colors vibrate into a sharp white, Justin Philibon throws a jab to the left arm of the Tigress. He's done it before, that move is infallible. But! The big street vendor looses the vitality of a yellow snake from her curves. Justin Philibon looks as pitiful as a penitent taking the holy wafer. His forearms are held, bent to the point of snapping, a sovereign strength lifts him and whirls him like in a hallucination, inches from the ceiling. Then and there comes the assault! Doudou-Ménar climbs on top of the counter. Her legs tortured by varicose veins, she soon crashes on the police pack. Her breasts come down more destructive than sacks of gravel. Notebooks, watches, teeth, pens, typewriter fly. Candied fruit, basket, purple shoes take off in all directions. Seven, ten are knocked against each other, like calabashes in a basket, and are flung to the four corners of the earth. In the lock of her armpits skulls roar in anguish like mariners surprised at sea by a hurricane. The lawmen vainly apply their murderous techniques against her fortified-with-yam-and-hard-cabbage fat. Forty years of ill-luck have solidified her muscles, seasoned her pugnacity, and, in the hot pincers of her arms or teeth, the suddenly limp police horde perceives the murderous intent of a resentment that knows no horizon.

(Solibo Magnificent used to tell me : "Oiseau de Cham, you write. Very nice. I, Solibo, I speak.

You see the distance? In your book on the water-mama,[1] you want to capture the word in your writing, I see the rhythm you try to put into it, how you want to grab words so they ring in the mouth. You say to me: Am I doing the right thing, Papa? Me, I say: One writes but words, not the word, you should have spoken. To write is to take the conch out of the sea to shout: here's the conch! The word replies: where's the sea? But that's not the most important thing. I'm going and you're staying. I spoke but you, you're writing, announcing that you come from the word. You give me your hand over the distance. It's all very nice, but you just touch the distance . . .")

From his desk where he was questioning three rastas in the hope that they would uncover charges against themselves on their own, Chief Sergeant Philémon Bouaffesse had heard a fishmarket-around-a-quarter-to-noon kind of uproar. He turned away from the rastas and raised an eyebrow. Eyes half-closed, two fingers on the typewriter, the Chief Sergeant concluded this laborious Q&A with an unexpected epiphany: something was going on in the hall! If he had been a vegetable, he would have naturally been a hot pepper, attracted to all sauces. Sending the rastas back to the holding pen in a great hurry, especially since they did have permanent addresses, didn't smoke marijuana, and seemed to have worn dreadlocks just for Carnival, our man went into the hall with the light footstep of a boss who wants to catch an employee screwing up. At the sight of the hullabaloo around Doudou-Ménar, he manifested his surprise

---

[1]*Manman Dlo contre la fée Carabosse* [*The watermama against Carabosse the fairy*], Ed. Caribéennes.

with only one of his favorite expressions, the one which, de-
fying all translation, vertiginously associates philosophical
peaks and abysses:

—Mothercrocker!

The son of Stéphanise Laguinée and Pierre-Jacques
Gros-Désors, he bore the surname of one called Bouaffesse,
a good blackman, though unable to resist the stale syrup of
quimbois that Stéphanise had mixed into his punch. Right
then and there, quivering with a sudden paternal fiber, the
good Bouaffesse went to recognize the latter's child at the
registry office. Once the name was obtained, Stéphanise
Laguinée advised the good man to go transpire under another sun, which he must have taken literally since he disappeared in his skiff, chasing after the dying day. For
Gros-Désors, the sire, the future Chief Sergeant became
only the sixteenth of the unrecognized children he fathered
every nine months, competing with his friends. The absence
of a father never seemed to traumatize our man (nor even
his eighteen half-brothers and -sisters) even though the psychologist (a very competent man from Auvergne) seemed
troubled when that little blackman would invariably reply
to the questions *Mother?* and then *Father?*: Stéphanise
Laguinée! . . . The scientist, poorly digesting the idea that a
mother could be so identified with the father, spent the rest
of his visit building theoretical bridges over the impasses of
the oedipal complex. What to say about the sergeant-to-be's
contribution to the development of ethno-colonial psychol-
ogy or about his responsibility in the massacres of women,
children, and the elderly—a specialty of his regiment in the
Algerian War—a few years later? And, since writing cannot be omniscient, no one can say for sure how he met the
woman of his life (a coolie, they say), nor why he made sure
she could give birth ten times before marrying her without
even the simplest dinner or party, nor even how he dumped

his naval jersey, in which he vegetated after the colonial war, for the official blues of a guardian of the peace. Moreover, all questions concerning how he became sergeant, then lieutenant, and finally chief sergeant without these promotions being accompanied by the usual exile in the frost of Parisian police stations are still unanswered. At the moment he entered the hall (and so, in a manner, the Solibo case), he was already feared by the black mafia of the town's most dangerous corners. They said that he had never blinked before a knife fight, nor shivered before the razor artists. The notorious murderers, the maniacs throwing bottles of acid, those animals who would enter into a happy trance at the mere sight of police, all those freaks who cut policemen to pieces in order to end colonialism, never gave him any trouble. Therefore it was a manly blackman (if not a great one), and a good policeman (if not a genius), who froze Doudou-Ménar and her pack of assailants with a simple: What on earth? You doing a funny-farm salsa here, or what?

There's a Kodak photo of Chief Sergeant Bouaffesse that came out on the front page of *France-Antilles,** a long time before Independence. He's standing by a recently dug-up coffin from which he's just extracted a lot of junk: tibias tied in a cross, pinned dolls, dried kid hearts . . . Called upon by the Syrian who discovered this hex in front of his shop, the lieutenant (not yet sergeant) had contained the turmoil by opening the coffin with his heel and emptying its contents with a serene hand. This case earned him the reputation of semi-quimboiseur, which he often used later to scare a few rebels. Before thinking about knifing him, one had, it is true, the tendency to think twice when he'd tranquilly warn: If you touch me with your blade you're going to cut your own flesh . . . What's more, when we tried to run away, without raising a finger he yelled: *Down!* And when Bouaffesse said *Down!,* like it or not, it was all the same: believe me, you got down, yes you did.

But that's not today's tale. Today's tale is about Bouaffesse's Kodak photo in *France-Antilles.* It explains why they call him Ti-Coca, Li'l Coke. He is short, massive, almost round like a bottle. In fact, you'd really think he was a good guy if he didn't have those shaggy eyebrows which add an extra visor to his cap, and that look in his two murderous agate eyes. In the picture: hands on hips, in one of his favorite poses, a sturdy foot on the coffin as in those old pictures of colonial hunts (probable objects of his admiration). What else is worthy of note? The mustache. Yes, the mustache. A maxi-mustache polished with a toothbrush, elegantly curled up at the ends like peculiar fish hooks. It is grayed today but still worthy of envy. One more thing: if one hollers, "Ti-Coca!" it's always behind in his back. Who'd dare do it to his face?

("Chamoiseau? Because for them you were the biblical Shem's descendant (thus, his bird . . .), the one with the black skin," Solibo used to tell me . . .)

In the hall, all remained suspended: Doudou-Ménar held and bound like a blinded opossum, the cops lined up stiffly like Saint Anthony candles on a humble tomb. In a calm more unsettling than anger, Bouaffesse walked up and down the battlefield, stopping at the debris, radiating an authority which his men and a thoroughly mussed-up Doudou-Ménar absorbed like flypaper. This man, it must be said, was made of the stuff of chiefs. On the slave ship he would have been the one to bathe us with seawater, to disinfect the hold with boiling vinegar, and to rub us with oil right before the sale. On the plantation he would have been the one to shout the cadence of the field work until he became overseer. He was made to be a chief, but on the winner's side. To lead a group of scabby maroons, for example, wouldn't have interested him. His step resounded gloomily on the tiles. The silence amplified the creaking of his uniform, in an ever-stretching moment fit for nervous breakdowns: lips trembled, temple veins throbbed, Doudou-Ménar noisily chewed nonexistent gum. The Chief Sergeant prolonged this tension to a nerve-wracking degree, then he spoke in a soft and low voice, not gentle but appeasing, which smoothed even the biggest bags of nerves present and submitted the assembly to his boot, making it more docile than an old blackman in the vicinity of a dog (and no stone in sight, man).

—What is it, huh? he said. (Which, translated into colonial French, would be something like: Might you explain to me what is at the origin of this deplorable situation?)

Solibo's in agony in the Savanna, murmured Doudou-Ménar. Like a true professional, Bouaffesse detected right then a gravity in her voice which had escaped the rest. Huh, who's in agony? . . . Turning around, he addressed the big woman. The latter was already casting upon him a defiant look straight out of the westerns, when, unexpectedly, eyes bulging, joy swallowed up her face: A-ah! Philémon, I didn't recognize you standing there like that, no! So, you're a policeman, a shit-guard,[1] huh? . . . At this heart-rending outburst, the Chief Sergeant thought her crazy, but being a ladies' man, expert in such enigmas, he went on red alert in order to avoid any oversight that might crimp his hand.

---

[1][This term originally referred to policemen guarding Fort-de-France's canals from the illegal dumping of slops.]

Therefore, he said nothing, since it is true that in certain circumstances, silence rectifies things better than an idiotic word. So then: mute observation while opposite him Doudou-Ménar fidgeted: You don't recognize me, Philémon? ... Oh, painful sudden recollection! Despite himself, the Chief Sergeant had to arch an eyebrow and force a smile: Holyshit! it's Lolita, he thought.

The night of his meeting with the young Lolita Boidevan rushed back to his memory. At the time a simple guardian of the peace, he justified (to his coolie concubine) his nocturnal absences with stories about Disaster Protocol Drills, and haunted the feminine fishponds of small parties, balls, and other events where the juices flowed. This particular night, he had chosen La Bananeraie, a trendy abode of love, where the Haitian orchestra of Nemours Jean-Baptiste played. After the first whiskey & coke watered with light beer (indispensable to avoid monkeying in front of the lady), he had crossed the hall, spotting some interesting heads among what he called "the cattle." He walked along the stage where the orchestra distilled "Ti-Manman chérie," navigated between tables in a studied stride which constituted the ritual of the kalior,* the ladies' man: to see and to be seen. Show off the tucked-in Pierre Cardin shirt open on a fleecy chest, the tiny Martinique charm at the end of a gold chain, and (oh yes!) the little cross cradled under the collarbone on a shorter chain. Show off the high-waist trousers, the fine leather belt, the pack of American cigarettes (local Mélias discredit you!) dangling from the fingertips of a hand heavy with bracelet and thick signet ring. While ambling about, smoke in long ecstatic puffs, twisting your wrist this way and that to show off the glistening watch. And don't forget to leave a fresh and tenacious trail: perfume is the signature of presence. The young Bouaffesse applied this technique with the faith of experience. But kaliors are sometimes faced with difficult days. Days when the balls attract only women with wigs, smelling of Vaseline and burnt hair, with red dresses and white-high-heel-shoes-size-eleven, talcum powdered, and who savagely refuse to dance if the guy doing the asking is darker than they are. Bouaffesse had light brown skin. There could be worse, but this time, for a kalior, there was also better. After three refusals, he was meditating upon these truths when an accessible creature appeared. Sitting alone near the orchestra, she sipped the singer with her eyes. He looked at the flounced gown: closely hugging what were still only simple curves. He looked at the shoes: black, with half-heels. He looked at the style: rose-painted lips, shining skin attenuated in powder, peasant style but nice. And last: a refreshing face with big innocent eyes that a drifting kalior couldn't ignore. The young Bouaffesse invited the young girl whose name he would soon learn was Lolita Boidevan, not knowing that a few years later she would be named Doudou-Ménar, a major troublemaker in Fort-de-France.

Winning her over was easy. A very respectable calypso mambo. Then a rumba in the course of which Bouaffesse executed the latest steps, bending his knees, chain bracelet jangling, cologne trailing. When Nemours Jean-Baptiste began to sing the "Ginette," then the "Dimanche matin" (which our musicians can keep up for so long it arouses envy), the young Bouaffesse began, as planned, brushing against her belly, tipping the Beauty, his forearms tight round her waist. The tipping part is crucial because, at the end, it delivers the coveted woman to the artiste. Bouaffesse respectably tipped her, two seconds before the end of the piece (you must calculate well), and thus could, without frightening his prey, gyrate his hips in the sexiest way. The melody finished, he bowed like a Chinaman and disappeared into the darkness of the room (the Chinese trick is a double one: it shrouds your voice in mystery, while singularly displaying gratitude). From a dark corner, Bouaffesse counted the dances, let three go by in order to condense the mystery, to make himself be desired and, especially, to wipe off the first sweat (in the course of the seduction, the kalior must not perspire). The decisive stage: you reappear, fresh, smiling, and invite from afar (always get her to walk toward you, son). Either she accepts, or she refuses. If she refuses: whiskey and light beer before going elsewhere to chase. If she accepts: bow very low with a little swing and take care to sound a bit hoarse (always works). Ladies and gentlemen, Lolita Boidevan accepted.

The Beauty was consumed in an air-conditioned Citroën, to the rhythm of a slow Otis Redding tune gliding from the hidden walls of some house. For Bouaffesse all had turned out for the best: the tipping, the wicked gyrations, the purring of a trained voice in the earlobe: What do your friends call you? hmm, Lolita, sweet, sweet, oh it's like sugar dancing with you . . . , Otis Redding, the seat pulled back. Bouaffesse delivered the deathblow by the seaside. The horizon yellowing over the oceanic uproar inspired a virile ardor in him, and his performances were urged not only by the hormonal urges of sleepless nights. Not to overpraise him, don't forget that he began with the Dominican salsa (a difficult one as you know) and that he finished with a Jump Jim Crow—all of which (if true) would indeed merit an international ranking; just like he claims during his precinct drinking binges.

There exists an art of fucking, of fugitive love. You seize the instant to be dazzling. It's compact, absolute love at first sight, a brevity which rejoins eternity. Doudou, we won't haul Time's net together, no one brings anything back from it: with Time, Time always wins, say the blackfolks around here. Bouaffesse (although he would have never admitted it to the coolie he put in a house with two or three children) agreed with this, and he lengthily explained it to the young lover still bewildered by the song of her flesh: I will never forget you . . .

—Neither will I . . . , Lolita had promised.

Doudou-Ménar kept her word.

> (Solibo Magnificent used to tell me: "Z'Oiseau, you say: Tradition, tradition, tradition . . . , you bawl on the floor for the tree that loses its leaves, as if the leaf was the root! . . . Leave tradition alone, son, and watch the root . . .")

Can one love so fleetingly? Can love be as brief as a drink after a game of dominoes? Shouldn't we dig a trench between what we get from the balls and what comes from the heart? That seduced woman with whom you draw the first milk of dawn—must you put her aside on your love-list just like you scatter peppers all over a marinated dish? And then, this country is too small: where can you keep a secret? . . . Some of this was going through Bouaffesse's head as he scrutinized Doudou-Ménar. Around him, his subordinates itched with impatience, so much so that the Chief Sergeant was shaken from his reverie (I recognize you, madame, join me in my office), got the place put back together, had the dirty men cleaned up, before explaining to the battered avengers that the lady in question was his cousin by an uncle's left hand, that this incident was deplorable, that it was always better not to raise the heat nor cut the pepper, that it was not exactly a do-me-a-favor, but if you don't report it I'll know how to take care of you better than the Credit Union. The pack fatly approved and left the same way it came, leaving Justin Philibon with his log-book . . .

—Put a period at the end of the lady's statement!

In his office, Bouaffesse understood a fourth of what she said: so, he summarized, he choked, right? If he yelled *Patat' sa!* and fell blip!, it might also have been because of some kind of dizziness, the kind pregnant women get maybe . . . He examined Doudou-Ménar, looking under the puffed-up face for the curves of the young woman, and, de-tail by detail, Lolita took shape in front of him despite the apocalyptic evidence of the breasts, the waist, the muscled arms. Under the salacious gaze of her ephemeral lover, the savage woman simpered with throaty sounds. When he touched her shoulder (while continuing his lecture about the kinds of dizziness there are, because you know there's rum dizziness, bad-liver dizziness, empty-balls dizziness, dizziness when you're not dizzy at all . . .), she undulated and shivered like a vine beneath the flight of a tree lizard and murmured: Oh Philémon, you still have hazel eyes, hmmm . . . The Chief Sergeant, already dazed, didn't say a word, but accentuated his caress.

It was the nocturnal habit of Bouaffesse to use his of-fice for the impromptu consummation of his love affairs. There are no words on Love around here. All these stones of affliction to chew are the reasons why words on Love have not found the right blackman. Our pre-literature is made up of screams, of hatred, of vindication, of prophecies at the inevitable Dawns, of analysts, of lesson givers, guardians of soluble solutions to the miseries of this world, and the black-folks this, and the blackfolks that, and the Universal, ah yes the Universal! . . . Conclusion: no song about Love. No song about sex. Negritude was a eunuch. And Antilleanity has no libido. They had lots of children (mostly illegitimate) but without any goddamn love. That's more or less what Justin Philibon might have said to himself if his readings had gone beyond the bloody columns of the *France-Antilles* newspaper, or even, and especially, if our scribe-scientists had written in order to be read by the people from around here. From his desk, he kept an eye on the closed door of Bouaffesse's office, while patching up the logbook. Jealousy stung his heart, he's going to fuck her for sure, no he's probably fucking her right now under my nose, what a dog! To do that in an office like an old white man, the boss is an asshole but he sure is good with women, he fucks everything that comes here at night, during the day he can't, but at night he fucks hard, I gotta get that scented goo he puts on his hair, beef gelatin with olive oil I hear, it softens the hair, oh yeah! I can even hear his voice, he must have jumped on her flwap! and tore her to pieces on the desk like a key opens a lock, it must be one of his old mistresses, good god! He's fucking her while I'm sitting behind the béké's counter like a cartoon character! . . . At the end of an eternity, he saw them come out of the office with clothes too well adjusted and eyes gleaming. Eyebrows braided like vetiver, the Authority came near the counter, checked the logbook and, with Doudou-Ménar in tow, ordered in a cold voice: Philibon, note that I am taking care of this matter and call the fire-and-rescue squad just in case . . .

Sitting in the back of the van with three policemen, Doudou-Ménar is fascinated. The country goes by in front of her, cut into lozenges by the grillwork protecting the dirty panes. It smells of the grease of weapons, cigarettes, the sour sweat of terrorized innocence. Careless bleaching has only slightly reduced all that, but the Fat One smells nothing. Between the police uniforms, she has broken into legitimate existence, suddenly realizing that she had been living like all of us, on the margins, on those paths which trace a country other than that of the colonial roads. Therefore, one must understand: in the van heading toward us and Solibo, Doudou-Ménar is legalized and proud.

Chapter 2

My friends!

Here the Chief Sergeant

brings back his wretched slappity-slap

and gets all of us in a pickle

(Tears for whom?

For Charlo', of course.)

At the end of the wee hours,[1] when Solibo Magnificent started giving off the heavy odor of death's first fumes, the company shook off its lethargy to figure the sun's height in the sky: Say dear God what time is it up there? Where's Doudou-Ménar? People got up, stretched, limped, rubbing pins-and-needles from their legs. Some bent over Solibo, now unrecognizable, bloated by death. Maria-Jésus Sidonise was sitting by him and hadn't stopped watching him for a second. Kneeling near the body, elbow on her sherbet maker, she seemed to have turned to stone, a cliff, deprived of her breathing warmth, her skin as flaccid as the Magnificent's. How terrible to see the two of them like this! Blighted like yams planted in the full moon, too bitter or too pulpy. My children, murmured Sidonise while we cast down our eyes, I tell you what the worst part is: his body should have already received a lemongrass bath, fresh on white sheets, under the light of his candles and the women's prayers, it would wear a cross, and we would have kept bath water under the bed until it was time to throw it on the hearse's wheels... Where is the lemon that blocks the fumes of the departed? ... Now Sidonise's whole bust swayed like a leaf in a melancholy alizé.* We cast furtive looks at the shards of her pain, and with heavy hearts we listened to her Creole voice in eulogy: There was a time I lived with Solibo, for many years, yes, he only came on Tuesdays and Sundays,

[1]["At the end of the wee hours," a specifically Césairean poetic formula, is the first line of *Notebook of a Return to the Native Land*. See *Aimé Césaire: The Collected Poetry,* trans. Clayton Eshlemam and Annette Smith (Berkeley: University of California Press, 1983).]

and stayed in my house without looking through the window. It's carrying on that way that we got two children. He was in and out of more than a few homes like most men from around here, but he brought the meat for the children. If times were bad and he hadn't a good sou left, he made sure we had the sea-given fish, the freshly picked vegetable. He went out of my life when I told him that Dalta the customs officer (a civil servant for real) had asked to live together with me, with God's blessing, paper from the city hall, and everything. He said: Maria girl, I am happy for you (but the light in his eyes became dim), come by the market to see me if you ever need anything . . . Oh, mama! Dalta's a good man, he was always good with the children, but my body's only got one season: Solibo. On Tuesdays and Sundays, Solibo made me laugh, laugh, laugh, not the little laugh you cough at the movies, but the one where you show all your teeth to the sun. He spoke to me, sang me pretty things, and showed me quadrille steps, always buzzing like a dragonfly after the first dew! . . . Even the boiled dasheen, flavored with a piece of cod, seemed like a baptism feast when I was with him: he lit my life like a lamp! After lunch, when the heat dripped from the tin roof, he put his hands on my hips: Oh here's my treasure! . . . , or he warbled: My good sugar-woman, what do you taste like today, huh? . . . , And I know I am going to make you all laugh now, when he was working up and down my flesh all serious, and my belly was taking flight, all the sudden he would exclaim: *Ooh! it fee-eels good, the békés get it every day, sure, but us black people just once a year!* . . . She interrupted her rocking in a chuckle-sob which silently ran through her body. Our sadness bowed before this shining wistfulness all her own.

Didon, master jobber at the vegetable market, came near Sidonise, touched her hair to say thank you, then straightening the knots in his shoulders, he raised his fore-head in order to clear his throat and give us a tale. Tight as a bud, his silhouette lumpy with knotty little muscles, a woman's earring bit one of his ears. Friends, here is my sadness, he said, allow me a memory or two ... We waited for someone else to conjure up an upright, comforting Solibo going about on one of his most beautiful days. We made mouth music and clapped to help him strengthen his voice ... Didon spoke like a deaf man, slow, in a Creole which often brought to mind Guadeloupe. His elocution, almost a monotone, slipped away on the wind, and you had to lean in to understand his words. When he finished talk-ing and sat down, the body returned to its painful present. But the extraordinary story of the long-one, the one that made Solibo known in distant villages, floated like a per-fume around us and all the way up to the top of the tree—simple as Didon said it:

The long-one had sprung out of a basket of weeds. Eyes sparkling, rustling, it stood up in the stall in front of Ma Goul, the oldest of the vendors. A long-one of the bad kind, you know, coiling with a black and yellow luster, moving quiet and strong. Seeing it in the middle of the mar-ket shook our hearts. Everyone quickly got out of there, leaving Ma Goul face-to-face with death in a deserted stall. The old woman was terrified. She opened her dull eyes and toothless mouth in an impossible scream. Already we had given up on her: the poor woman would leave life stupidly, burned by the poison of our oldest enemy. Some women twisted rosaries and prayers, rubbed magic seeds, or bawled away. We jobbers stood stuck like engines without oil. Friends, if you knew how much *the long-one scares us.* It has killed so many of us in the fields, its reptile curves carry so many ancient meanings that its very presence empties us.

Ma Goul was glued before the hissing death, like a fly trapped in the spider's lace. And the same went for us. That's when Solibo Magnificent came forward.

O sweetness for the eyes!

It's a memory that I comb over and over: what a sweet memory! . . . I saw him walking without moving the wind to meet Ma Goul on death's ground. When he stopped at the old woman's side, the snake imperceptibly pointed toward him. Solibo started to drone, he spoke, yes, but from afar it sounded like the bumblebee approaching a flower. Right then and there, we felt that things had changed: there was no hunter and no prey, but—forgive me everyone, I want to say it the way I saw it—but two hunters! In the market, at high noon, near Ma Goul resurrected, there were *two snakes!* . . . That's what made it a real circus, yes! How can I tell you what it was like? Vertigo? Head upside down? The Magnificent seized the long-one with one hand. He stuffed it in a bag and whispered some silent words as he carried it away. They say that he freed it in the Tivoli bushes. They also say that Ma Goul, an old woman deserving respect herself, from then on called him *Papa,* with a hand on her heart . . .

(Solibo used to tell me: "Oiseau de Cham, I will never drown. In water, I become water, before the wave I am wave. I will never burn myself either, because fire does not burn fire. And regarding that tale of the long-one that you're talking about, I don't remember the incident. But it's not impossible. Each creature is but a chord which you just have to tune in to . . . Stop scribbling scritch-scratch, and listen: to stiffen, to break the rhythm, is to call on death . . . Ti-Zibié, your pen will make you die, you poor bastard . . .")

Some lowered their eyelids, hanging on to the safe echo of the tales. Others looked across the Savanna, which was glowing with a dew the blackbirds had come to drink. Of the joy of Carnival only ruins and stains, dried-up bottles, bits of masks, shapeless old shoes lying around . . . I hadn't lived through the circus of the long-one—the market boils with so many stories! . . . —and it escaped me all the more because I looked so hard: to stare is to stop seeing; the eyes explore little by little, the way grasshoppers eat—eating only where they land. I had heard the story once, twice, three times, different versions, when I had asked the old women about the origin of the Magnificent and about the meaning of his nickname. Around here, we say *solibo* to designate the fall. Every blackman, and the blackwomen more often than their due, have had their solibo. The man who would become one of our great storytellers was shaken from youth's branches by the death of Amédé, his father—a brave blackman, a little greasy, with a pregnant woman's belly and a resounding voice that his son would inherit. He had come to Fort-de-France, like all of us, when the fields fed only ants and békés. The Germans hadn't succeeded in breaking his back during the time he had gone to save de Gaulle, but the roughnecks of Fort-de-France did. Amédé died in Morne*-Pichevin, right after pitifully cheating at serbi, leaving his wife, Florise, and his boy in a situation that was worse than death. Florise was no Amazon. When she tried to grab fate's fickle finger, it always slipped away. She never took hold of her destiny. Life for her was *squalor,* the indescribable kind that makes your life taste more bitter than a poorly leached manioc.* The unlucky woman soon lost it all and had to be taken to Colson Hospital when tafia and pain made her mind jump off the rails. Her boy vanished from life's traffic. They say he roamed the hills of Fort-de-France, where the grass-of-the-seven-paths marks off the deep woods. He haunted the shores of the Madame River up to Pont-de-Chaînes where the river becomes a canal. He ate soursops, mango, sometimes even these manger-coulis,* and drank from waterfalls whose tenant, the crayfish, he would grab and roast in the flame. It's our maroon way of life, those hours when the blackman from around here beholds in his conscience only that echo of himself (a moment favored by the musical silence of the woods) that has helped him become what he was. Of that time he has told me nothing except that he spoke to the stones and the bark, and that always, always, he looked in his chest for the breath that feeds the rustling of the leaves. When he reappeared in the town streets, a long time afterward, hairy, haggard, he fell into the vices of all drifting blackmen. A few old women at the market where he parked his distress named him Solibo, Creole for *blackman fallen to his last peg—and no ladder to climb back up.* As is done in such situations, the old women on lunch breaks offered him tales, oh words of survival, stories of street smarts where the charcoal of despair watched small flames triumph over it, tales of resistance, all the ones that the slaves had forged on hot evenings so the sky wouldn't fall. Many a man gone adrift had heard them, and no child from around here escaped them, but in Solibo it all sprouted, spread with more splendor than the red blossoms of the May peacock tree—so the old women, realizing this, increased the dose. Soon (Florise, his mother, had left Colson to sell milk to the soldiers of the Rochambeau barracks), he became a nice young man, full of a happy dignity that could attract anyone. They say his words were beautiful and knew the road to all ears, the invisible double doors which open on the heart. Furthermore, he mysteriously distilled the tales in such a way that he seemed to have derived their innermost meanings from himself. It was an old storyteller, a serious talker, who upon hearing him at the market one

Saturday pronounced him Magnificent. He refused the title for a long time: No way! Call me Solibo . . . Just Solibo . . . But the two words stuck together.

I stood up. Helped by the others who braced my voice by hand or by mouth, I spoke these words near Solibo's body. Sucette filled the silence of my pauses with a quivering groan by sliding his finger on the drumskin. Congo, La Fièvre, Charlo', and Bête-Longue murmured like in a quiet mass: *Share your wonderful stories with us, share them with us . . .*, while Sidonise and Conchita clicked their tongues, assented by closing their eyes and bowing their heads. All of that kept us warm, embraced the tree, the body of the Magnificent, and dissolved in the expanse of the Savanna. No one shed a tear. Grief was the mule that brought our memories on its back. But then, death retreated inch by inch, flowing through our hearts, or else we saw it with new eyes, as the natural last stage of all life, a necessary departure. When I sat down, after silence had dug a new abyss, Charlo' got up in his turn and, touching the Magnificent's forehead, apologized for not having thought to bring his sax. The slow cadence of our clapping, our heavy whispering, forced him to find in himself, without any instrument, a gift of remembrance . . . I only saw him once, said Charlo' in a city Creole. It was on Christmas Day, around Fort-de-France, at Ma Gnam's house where we had a pig which refused to die. At this time, people still raised pigs in their backyards. Hygiene wasn't an official thing yet, and so no blackman ever came into your home to forbid this or that for fear of fevers and mosquitoes. So Ma Gnam was going out of her mind, completely losing it with this animal. The pig was mad. Nothing could calm it down, neither the tafia-soaked bread, nor the here-piggy-piggy with the coochicoo, not even blows from a metal rod. It had broken a white mahoe rope and a bananamahoe one too. Even I, who had come as the bleeder, despite my experience, I was shocked and helpless. It seemed to me that this Christmas was going to be a terrible one. All year, Ma Gnam had fattened the pig which was now poisoning its flesh with fear and folly. That's when she called one of her sons: Souris, go get Mr. Solibo for me . . . Thinking she was getting another Christmas pig-bleeder, I put on a sour face and was about to leave. Where are you off to, Charlo'? Ma Gnam had called me back, Mr. Solibo isn't some other bleeder, but a wordsman . . . I couldn't see what would be the use of that then, but I kept my mouth shut. Souris came back right away with Mr. Solibo. He had picked up the man at the market where the latter sold charcoal, I think. In his flour-sack clothes and old panama hat he didn't look too good. Short, with long arms, he stuck out his head in front of him like a box turtle. When my eyes met his and he touched my shoulder (You there, son?), when he kissed Ma Goul, lifting his hat and asking for his throat's winy due, I began to sense his power. His voice vibrated in his skull, in his cheeks, danced in his eyes, his chest, and his belly: Strength. He hadn't even peeked into the yard when that Master Pig stopped squealing. He jumped into the yard to talk to the animal which was still running around. Then, there it lay on one side, dizzy. Mr. Solibo talked to it while around my knife its heart slid into exile in the basin: dead without realizing it, with the flesh nice and pink. I was s-t-u-n-n-e-d! I don't remember what he said to the pig, but even without words or stories, Solibo was a Voice before the animal. And so when I play the sax, and when I want to breathe a sound that spits fire, I relive that day in my mind, I replay the do ti la sol of his voice. When I succeed, but it doesn't happen every day you know, everyone always says it was real pretty that sax piece, Charlo' boy! . . .

(Papa, two questions, I had said to Solibo a
long time after the incident with Ma Gnam's pig:
How can talk calm a mad pig? and isn't it ludicrous to use it to kill a pig? ... The Magnificent
had smiled: "You have to be what you do, pig
before the pig, pig words for pig squeals, lose
your importance, and then all words will calm.
Now Chamzibié, you say: Ludicrous. Pretty
French. You, you weep for a slaughtered pig, and
I had pity on Ma Gnam's misery and her seven
children's Christmas . . .")

Standing between the roots, Charlo' contemplated the
body as if he had just discovered it. His words had aroused
so many echoes in himself . . . Tall, his belly collapsing above
his long legs, the bags beneath his eyes stored his tally of
drinks and sleepless nights. In the Savanna, after drinking
to their heart's content, blackbirds picked at some invisible
thing in the heart of the field. Some of the dew still shone
but the wind was no longer so cool. Congo's good ear caught
the police van well before it was audible. *Mi la hopo,* here
come the police! he said in the tone one uses to signal the approach of dogs. No one understood the warning and the police van jumped into the memorial's midst (Goodgod! the
police . . .), making our hearts j-j-jump . . . O friends, who
here is at ease when the police are around? Who swallows
his rum without choking or shivering? With cops, the hunting dogs from slavery days return, the maroon-chasing
dogs, the militia that watched the plantation, the overseers,
the mounted guards, the Vichy marines of the time of the
Admiral, all one and the same Force inscribed in the collective memory under the unique attestation of our history:
Coppers! here come the poliiice!

The van of the Law stopped by the tamarind tree. Vlam-vlam! The right front door and the two in the back are thrown open. Chief Sergeant Bouaffesse and three acolytes jump out. The van hiccups. The hand brake creaks energetically. The driver comes out in turn. Then, not a sound. Only the flash of the rotating beacon. Shaken by the maneuver, Doudou-Ménar emerges staggering: Hey, mister! say, you got your license from a Crackerjack box? she yells to the driver. She is ready to ignite, but the Chief Sergeant cools her anger: Peace, woman! . . . The company, piled up around Solibo, shivers. Oh Lord, it's Ti-Coca in person heading here! . . . All suddenly realize the danger of their predicament: there they are early in the morning, standing by a dead body for no good reason, and here comes a chief sergeant savage and mean . . . Already, one or two try to make themselves scarce, slowly shuffling their feet to find a way out. Bouaffesse, who seems to have guessed their intention, hands on hips, surrounds the little group with his eyes: Stay where you are, if you please, if you don't want things to get unpleasant! . . . We stand still, more stopped than in a photo frozen in the sweat of life's worst moments. The four lawmen circle us slowly, like red wasps. Bouaffesse resolutely approaches Solibo's body: Hey there, get up, get up! . . . Of course, no surprise, Solibo does not move. The Chief Sergeant pushes him with his foot and comes back toward us: Is he drunk or what? . . . Our eyes stray, no one says jack, Bouaffesse keeps staring at us. One of his men also goes to check the body, he paws at it feverishly, then vlap! boing! jumps, eyes bulging, aiming his gun at us: Hands up! my trigger's sensitive! . . . The Chief Sergeant raises a disconcerted eyebrow. He is surprised. With a careful slowness he turns to the cowboy, who crumples his cap to

wipe his brow, hops, shuffles to keep his line of sight unob-
structed by his Chief Sergeant.

—Hey Bobé, worries Bouaffesse, what's with you?

—The corpse is dead, chief, yells Bobé—hysterical.

The Chief Sergeant metamorphosed.[1] The wings of
his nose fluttering, wrinkles arched around his lips, belly
tucked in, back held straight by an invisible lead thread, he
threw us oh Lord! a look which is better left unmentioned.
While Bobé screwed up his eyes for an unforgivable shot,
and the other three tightened the circle around us, the Chief
Sergeant went back to the body, this time probably in his official capacity. Ruffled like a goose, he observed the scene:
the tree, the roots, Sucette's drum, the demijohn, our small
pharmaceutical bottles. He seemed like an anxious night-
walker, watching all the paths that retreat coiling farther
and farther away from a silk-cotton tree's malefic shadow.
He had even taken out a small notebook and begun scribbling this-and-that with such seriousness that everything in
the place looked bigger and seemed more suspicious. Wow!
it really is possible to sweat buckets without climbing up
Gros-Morne. Our hearts pumped up an inexplicable guilt,
beating even faster when the Chief Sergeant examined this
or that bit of trash, and marked scritch-scratch I don't know
what. Then he plunged into an endless examination of the
body, turning around from time to time to fix us a look
which was enough to freeze our toes and balls. He hadn't
stumbled across a suspicious body in a long time. Ordinarily,
there was no hide-and-seek. The victim would be mince-
meat and, cutlass in hand, the killer would still be cursing
the body when the police arrived at the scene. Or a girl-

---

[1]Or *mofwaza,* if that's any help.

friend would have thrown scalding water on her lover and would demand to see a judge so she could tell him why she did this to her Octave . . . The bodies would often be cray-fishermen caught and drowned under a treacherous rock, or a man hanged by misfortune, or a woman swollen by the poison that a disappointed love inspires, an old man stewed in his tafia, an unintentionally (but officially) teargassed demonstrator. His last suspicious body—which by the way remained so since it was a dorlis* victim (what can the white man's law do with a sorcerous crime?)—was four years ago. So, before this unexpected, open-eyed corpse, as stiff as lard in cold soup, with its arms raised in an *oh hallelujah,* the Chief Sergeant is a bit confused. Sure, he knows that he's supposed to take certain measures and avoid major fuck-ups, that any little thing can get him promotion or hell. Bits of police correspondence courses come dribbling back to him. Preserve all evidence, all traces, erase no footprints, accurately mark the body's position, keep the place in its original state, and above all preserve—yes, but what? . . . not even a piece of brain lying around that I could slip into a plastic bag . . . Only the debris of rum suckers celebrating Carnival, dust, and dried tamarinds! . . . what's that stain? . . . juice or what? . . . let's take notes . . . sweet-jumpin'-Mary-and-Joseph! the body doesn't even have a scratch! . . . is this a bloodless blackman? . . . They kill him and he doesn't bleed? . . . not possible, everyone's got blood, even the Haitians! . . . he looks like a drowned man, yes that's it, a drowned man, let's write that down . . . wait, if I write that they're going to ask me: where's the water? . . . it's true, you don't drown by a tamarind tree . . . so what is it? . . . they must have killed him with rat poison . . . he's already stiff, yes . . . Arrgh! what should I do?

. . .

Worrisome thing: he was walking toward us and looked as if he had made up his mind about something. The group of imbeciles now regretted having hung around all bunched up together as if to protect themselves from a cold wind. Losing interest in his aim, Bobé (Robert Dité's his name, the son of his Ma Dité and some black runaway) now only busied himself with his drooling. The three other policemen (the name of the first was Figaro Paul, legendary for his long-lasting grudges and underhand vengeance and thus nicknamed Diab-Anba-Feuilles; Doussette Mano was the name of the second, his sobriquet was Nono-Golden-maw because of his glittering denture; the last one was Salamer Cyprien, also known as Jambette, probably because of the way he handled the knife he carried around hidden in a handkerchief) shivered, so attentive were they to an order to apprehend which wasn't coming fast enough.

—So, gentlemen?! Now is when you call us, when this body's been dead-dead for a while now, huh?

The voice of the Chief Sergeant crackled like a bamboo fire. Breaking the nice arch of his mustache, a murderous grimace betrayed the stumps of his teeth. The company drew together again, dumbfounded. Bouaffesse, like a careful toreador, was circling it when ooowiie-ooh-wou! the fire-and-rescue squad's red ambulance arrived. The flashing lights conferred such a climate of catastrophe on the place that some curious passersby, left out by life, came around with one question buzzing on their lips: What's going on? what's going on? *ô sa ki ni?*

Without asking anyone, two fire-and-rescuemen pull out their stretcher and break into a hundred-meter dash toward the body. *What are you doing?* yells Bouaffesse. Diab-

Anba-Feuilles and Jambette, promotion in mind, understand their chief's every word before he finishes saying it. Linking arms, they try to hook the stretcher bearers. But being professionals, the latter instinctively dodge past them and resume their race. Sticking his foot out, Jambette makes one of them trip and crash, mouth swarming with insults that Nono-Goldenmaw and Bobé inexplicably assume are meant for them. *Repeat what you just said!* they explode in unanimous rancor, clubs in the air. The first stretcher bearer turns around. He beholds his colleague's bloody face. Panic grips him and he lifts the stretcher as if using a pole to get at a ripe fruit. Pow!! Diab-Anba-Feuilles gets one of the handles in the eye and howls with pain, getting in the way of Bobé, Nono-Goldenmaw, and Jambette. All tangle and crash in a blogodo of dust. The toothless fire-and-rescueman emerges and runs toward the ambulance looking for a tire jack. On his way, he rouses the other two who had been standing petrified by the ambulance: *Yo lé tjwé nou,* they want to kill us! . . . Now the three of them plunge back into the mêlée. Jambette, forgetting all police dignity, has taken out his famous handkerchief with the knife, zip! zip! slashing the ventral side of the uniform of one of the fire-and-rescuemen. A bit of trickling blood, and the latter yells as if being lynched: The Law makes people bleed, *La Lwa ka senyen moun!* . . . Amazing revelation, terrifying too, judging by its effects: the fire-and-rescuemen leave the battle zigzagging through the Savanna: *La Lwa ka senyen moun!* . . . So suddenly, curious onlookers who until now had been eating up the spectacle decide to leave. Bouaffesse is frozen before the disaster: evidence, traces, and the "scene in its original state" swirl around in his head. Blah blah blah, Doudou-Ménar, hands on her hips, finds something to yak about despite the thick dust. The fire-and-rescuemen on the run have formed a semicircle and are returning to their vehicle. But it seems that

Jambette and Bobé, Diab-Anba-Feuilles and Nono-Golden-maw most certainly see in that move only a vengeful assault, since they get their guns out: I want the one in the middle, I'll go to jail for him! . . . *Put that away!* Bouaffesse belts. Raising an appeasing arm, he stands between his men and the fire-and-rescuemen, who converge again and—if you can believe it, even better—calm down as he speaks.

Doudou-Ménar's blah blah blah was choked off by such a show of authority. The policemen had put away their deadly toys but remained vigilant. We huddled together more tightly, fearing the return of a cold wind. Gentlemen of the fire-and-rescue profession, accept our apologies, the Chief Sergeant ordered; we called you because the body, here present, was supposed to be just passed out but has since become a murdered person . . .
Lord!
Ave Maria!
Saint Michael, give us a little hand!
The word *murdered* cast upon us the seven kinds of affliction: the trembling, the mushy knees, the pounding heart, the bulging eyes, the frozen marrow, red rashes without itching, white rashes with itching. We ran to the four corners of the earth. We hadn't even landed on the Savanna's grass when Bouaffesse yelled: *Hey!* . . . (What the hell is *Hey!?* A vine or a lasso? Glue or a brake?) Abruptly halted, we stood hopeless, droopy eyes, slouched back. *Line up these people!* ordered Bouaffesse, whose implacable cruelty seemed to pour into the dark red of his gaze. His men lined us up, turning off the attentive fire-and-rescuemen's anger with the spectacle of our misery. The one whose blood had pearled under the slashed uniform nonetheless kept some apprehension in his pocket. Things started to turn sour for Doudou-Ménar who, still believing herself legitimized,

looked as if she would approach her sergeant-lover. Will you please kindly explain to me what you think you're doing, Ma What's-Your-Name? croaked the lover whose voice seemed to deny most recent memories. Doudou-Ménar shuddered but insisted: Oh Philémon? ..., provoking the forgetful one to reprimand her: Line yourself up with the other suspects, if-you-pleeze! ... The Tigress regained her self-control in a few seconds and, bust arched, eyelids concealing a murderous look, she inquired in a dangerously sweet voice: Pleeze, I'm not sure I understand what's going on, on whom have you unleashed this gamut of words, huh? ... Perceiving a threat, Diab-Anba-Feuilles rushed forward between his chief and the formidable street vendor. He held his club carelessly in his hand, but his shaking betrayed the eruption of anger which generally preceded his police exploits.

Stay out of this, li'l man! orders Bouaffesse, who isn't afraid. But Diab's eyes are already locked on Doudou-Ménar's. A silent confrontation of two fighters, sizzling pepper on a hot pan. The two troublemakers have sized each other up, nothing you can do now. Even Bouaffesse steps back. He expects imminent disaster and can't help but salivate at the idea of battered heads that look like stuffed crabs. The rising thirst to see the fight (oh yes we love these acmes of blood, that ever-flourishing violence that needs neither a how nor a why) dissipates the witnesses' fright. Doudou-Ménar has raised her head. She tries to dominate Diab-Anba-Feuilles who, however, is taller than she. Shivering, the latter tries to get her to go back in the line but, stiff and breathless, Doudou-Ménar plants herself. I've got something for you, she spits out at him.—You ... you ... you don't know who I am? Diab-Anba-Feuilles fumes, if you don't know who I am, just ask around, Devil is what they call me, and I am the worst thing that ever happened to you,

you got that? a nightmare, and if I start fighting with you it's to the death, until I drop over your body, for I am ready to die, oh Jesus give me the last rites, I am going to die over her dead body! *sé mô man lé mô!* it's a real-real death I want! You've already made a circus at the police station and you want to start again here too? Well, here you mistake a 6 for a 9, I'm not Philibon, you know, I am the Devil, I've already filled thirteen graves at the Trabaut Cemetery. And if the poor blackmen and coolies could have been buried in the Richfolks' Cemetery, well then I'd have done my plantings at the Richfolks' Cemetery too! Go line up right now! Just because I'm wearing the police blues of the Law you think: Oh yeah he's probably an auntie! ... Well, I'm no auntie, I'm no auntie, just you see if I'm an auntie ... —and he brings his fist to his mouth (snap!), bites himself (hramph-grmn!) and shakes his head with rage tearing up his skin. A-ah! lips open on a set of bloody teeth, he holds his wound out before his prey: Did you see that? he growls, bloody skin between his teeth, you saw that? *aprézan zafê tjou'w,* from now on it's going to be hell for you: FOR YOU I HAVE BLED! ... Everyone is frozen. The fire-and-rescuemen move back. Those of us standing in line are seized by fright again. Bouaffesse has raised an eyebrow and flutters his eyelids: he's no longer enjoying this. Diab-Anba-Feuilles's freak show slightly lacks official dignity. The bleeding trick, that's thug behavior, not that of a police officer, Diab, calm down pleeze, you're on duty, not raping and pillaging on your own time! ... —Chief, don't get mixed up in this, squeals the mad policeman, I have bled for her now ..., and with his club he hits Doudou-Ménar, who doesn't see it coming, the meanest bash in police history—I still weep over it.

Christ! No one saw the billyclub fly up and crash down on her head. The policeman's body was arched as if an electrical charge ran through it, and there and then the fat vendor stumbled at his feet, head bathed in blood. The rest, on the other hand, we saw only too well. Rolled up on Diab-Anba-Feuilles's state-subsidized shoes, Doudou-Ménar twitched about, arms wrapped around her head. The blood splashed on her neck and shoulders. Her madras scarf had flown off, liberating permed, now sticky hair. Hovering over her, Diab-Anba-Feuilles was trying to keep his balance. His eyes were swirling, and his frothy mouth let out a torrent of ever-vibrant curses in a Creole he could no longer hold back: *Man sé an makoumê? ès man sé an makoumê? mi oala ou défolmanté akôdi sé koko siklon fésé, han! man sé pilonnen'w atê-a la, wi! man sé grajé'w kon an bi manyôk ek pijé'w anba plat' pyé mwen pou fè'w ladjé sos fyelou! ou modi! oala man menyen'w ou modi! pon labé pé ké tiré'y ba'w é dyab ké ayé oute zo'w yonn aprélot! mé ansé an jan mentsiyen, man grafyen'w ou pwézonnen! fwa'w pwézonnen! koudoun-ou pwézonnen! dréséguidup anpé ba'w fifin bout'la . . .* [I'm an auntie? so I'm an auntie? here you are like a coconut tree whipped by a hurricane, huh! Me I'm going to pound you into the ground, yep! I'm going to grate you like a piece of manioc and pound your spine with my heel into a sauce for rice! You're cursed! where I touch you, you're cursed! There isn't a thing that can get you out of the grip of the Devil who's going to break your bones one by one! I've got superpowers, and I'll poison your soul, your body, your sex! Come on, get up so I can finish you off right here!][1]

---

[1][*Chamoiseau's footnoted translation of the insults:*] Am I a coward? Am I a coward? here you are like a coconut tree devastated by a hurricane! Oh, I would like to walk all over you! you are cursed! Now that I have touched you, your body, your liver, your sex are under my curse! No sacrament can help that now! you're cursed! get up so I can finish you off!

. . .

The witnesses no longer stood in line. They gathered in a shapeless grape-bunch where bodies and heads no longer matched. Fright kept them all in ghostly silence. Nono-Goldenmaw, Jambette, and Bobé, disregarding the spectacle of Diab-Anba-Feuilles's anger, viciously patrolled the vicinity in order to dissuade the least intervention. Bouaffesse's wild-beast look denied his apparently complicit immobility. In fact, faced with a currently inaccessible Diab-Anba-Feuilles, he waited for the right moment when an imperial order could restore to Diab the little reason he had left. In the event, he used another powerful tactic: the official civil status of the crazed one and a French-French (Monsieur Figaro Paul, if-you-pleeze, you are forgetting yourself!), at which sound Diab-Anba-Feuilles became a statue, and were he not shaking like a poisoned cat, I would have described him: immobile.

The restored calm underscored the disaster. The Chief Sergeant wiped his temporal sweat, sighed his *Mothercrocker!* of difficult moments. Diab-Anba-Feuilles, bloody club at his feet, was unresponsive. His colleagues had once again lined up the witnesses, and stood at attention by our sides for reasons which were certainly qualified top secret. The fire-and-rescuemen were bustling over Doudou-Ménar. In a nervous silence which unveiled their anxiety, they bandaged the vendor's skull with the precious gestures of a starving man unearthing a yam. Careless of the refinements of that art, Bouaffesse was insisting: Get her up! ... The fire-and-rescuemen unanimously replied: This booboo's too serious for us, chief, she needs the hospital! ... After his evidence had vanished and the scene of the crime was in a complete state of disarray (things he knew, without having to ponder long over it, could have his career finish up in the Parisian cold), the Chief Sergeant resisted the idea of letting go an apparently essential witness. The smartest of the fire-and-rescuemen intervened. I don't want to force big words upon you, Sergeant, but the lady fell and she's got a cranial hemorrhage. It's a big medical word which might seem complicated to you, but it's really simple, it just means that the lady's head is like a stuffed tomato . . . This explanation provoked hesitation in the men of Law: the Chief Sergeant ran his fingers through his mustache, his men respectfully stared at the fire-and-rescueman. But Bouaffesse soon found the energy to make a clear-cut decision: Gentlemen of the fire-and-rescue, please come here, voilà, first I am going to present you with the apologies of the French Republic and my own, a few bops were given and received here and there, that wasn't mean, it warms one up, heh? Somebody's been murdered, as I have already explained it to you, you see him, no? the Penal Code and other texts state that all evidence must be preserved. Anyone who destroys a piece of evidence goes straight to jail! You understand that? so in the name of the Code and of the Republic, I should send you to jail, poof! because you have walked over footprints, but I am a nice guy, no one is supposed to disregard the Law but the Law comes from France and by the time it gets to this country, even if one knows it one does not have to enforce it all the time, you get it? So I've decided to leave you alone, and if you ever need anything stop by the police station and ask to see me, however if you try to file a complaint against me, annoy the District Attorney and make him digest his steak-fries badly, well then, I will take care of you personally. If you're going to put on a show then I'll be part of it too. If you bring the Pinder Circus then I'll be standing at the door to give out the tickets myself and I'll be your four hungry lions! . . . oh it's only a mischievous supposition, you got beaten up a little, but you're among friends, now take the stuffed tomato to the hospital. Goldenmaw, go with them and don't lose sight of the lady for a second because she's a witness who mustn't vanish, tell the medics not to leave her in a coma 'cause there's a criminal inquiry which needs her to be up, very well, good-bye gentlemen, rid me of her! ... —so that's how Doudou-Ménar woke up in the emergency room. She caused the usual turmoil which I will describe to you only so you can see why for a few hours, unlike Solibo, she seemed immortal ...

Note that under the tamarind tree, fifty-six manioc ants are marching on Solibo's body. It is their hour: the second half of the morning, with the night already far behind, all dew drunk up, shadows curling about the feet of everything, and a hot wind.

The Chief Sergeant took out his pad and approached the witnesses: I'm all ears! .... Penpoint to paper, he wasn't really looking at anyone, but everyone felt in various places the oppressive weight of his vigilance. The Chief Sergeant walked along the mute line and chose his first victim: Last name, first name, age, address, and occupation, pleeze! ... The witness replied in a falsely cheerful tone: Charlo', chief! Don't you remember me? I play music ... at the last police ball ... —His momentum was shattered by Bouaffesse's exasperation: You tell me Charlo', Charlo', what the hell is Charlo'? Charlo' de Gaulle? Charlo'magne? Charlo' who plays in the funny movies without ever opening his mouth even though we paid for the movie? you so famous you don't need a last name, huh? ... —With a more measured tone, Charlo' declared his name to be Charlo' Gros-Liberté, dropped off on this earth by his mother forty-four years ago, gave his age and residence as rue du 8-Mai in the city of Dillon. When Bouaffesse asked him: What kind of work you do for the béké?,[1] very much at ease, he confided: I'm the sax in the Combo Band orchestra, chief . . .

—Untrue! Diab-Anba-Feuilles, who had recovered, revealed perfidiously, the Combo Band went under last year!

Pen in the air, the Chief Sergeant loosed upon Charlo' an infernal look: Thus, you are the blower in an orchestra which doesn't exist any more?! You, all alone, you're the Combo? Me, I ask you nicely what you do for the béké, you you tell me you play sax but the orchestra is invisible? And when you play, you become invisible too, is that it? . . . — Thick and greasy laughs: All were displaying molars. It was good to appreciate Bouaffesse's humor, and even better that he knew it. Charlo', because of his position, overdid it: twisting, hands over his belly, each corner of his eyes inundated by twelve crayfish tears, he rolled ho ho ho in the dust. However, wisdom warns: *Too much salt spoils the soup!* The Chief Sergeant smashed his stick on Charlo's loins yelling: You ready for a party, but me, you mock me! . . . Thrown upright on his feet, laughter-choked, all in a muddle, Charlo' twisted around, trying to soothe the burning on his back with his hand: What did you do to me here, chief? Ow! you're losing it . . . *Shut up!* yelled Bouaffesse—and, at forty-four years of age, at a time when his mother no longer threatened him with it—his father never dared—and no béké would have used it at this hour in the fields, Charlo,' who cannot believe the pain, receives SISSAP! a slap.

Let me say a couple of things about Bouaffesse's slaps, known to everyone up to Grand-Rivière, where any old man who hasn't even ever been in town can tell you about

---

[1]Lands, factories, and the structures of economic production (direct or indirect) belonged to the békés. Whatever one's function, one worked for the békés. The expression has stayed on, inasmuch as things have evolved little.

them. One of them told me that our man spent a Good Friday night in a vault (*kyrie eleison*), hands soaking in a rotting coffin. He also says that at dawn, Bouaffesse sprinkled incense on them,[1] and that's why when he raises a hand at you, you're about to get one good whack from the grave. So I was told, and so I am telling you now, but unh-unh! don't attach my name to such sorts of stories.

Charlo', at first surprised, can no longer hold back his tears, they stream down his cheeks and die at the neck of his shirt. What else could he have done? After such a slap, you can only cry over the deathly rash which won't go away. Terrorized, the witnesses prefer to imagine themselves running away into the cloudy distance lit by the sun. The impassive Chief Sergeant has taken his notebook out again and growls: ... who killed Solibo? ... This interrogation quickly dries Charlo's tears. His mouth giving off bad breath, he only finds the strength to lament, bewildered: Killed Solibo? ... Killed Solibo?

Bouaffesse was about to continue with the dreadful question when he discovered twenty curious passersby heading toward the body in search of a western plot. *Where are you going, my gentlemen?* ... The curious ones, frightened, kept themselves at fifty meters. Others thought it wiser to pick their asses up, leave, and read all about it in *France-Antilles*.

—Jambette, cover the body with something, will you?

Jambette went to look for something in the van and brought back a few pieces of dirty cardboard which he was about to lay on the body. Someone was indignant: *Héti han-*

---

[1] Or dirtied them in yam holes.

man mwen pou'y houê ha anka houê la-a?! Pou hespé alô?! . . .[1]
Bouaffesse started. Pen in hand like a sword, he walked
along the line of suspects: Who spoke? Who just spoke? . . .
While Diab-Anba-Feuilles began to quiver once more and
Bobé was moving a cowboy hand to his gun, Jambette dis-
creetly took out his handkerchief again. *Who just spoke?*

—Sé'm, I did!

And the Chief Sergeant saw a freak of a blackman, his
eyes from another, old, backward world, cutting a pathetic
figure: Congo. The old man stood up before the policeman,
his arms raised in a gesture of poignant refusal: *Pon houn ni
dwa hê Holibo ha,* No one has the right to humiliate Solibo
this way! . . . The old man took off his shirt, his trousers, his
undershirt, unfolded his handkerchief, and held them out
to a Bouaffesse dumbfounded to see the old man's eyes fog
up with tears, demanding in a broken voice that they be
used to cover the body. The Chief Sergeant took the clothes
with a mechanical gesture, still staring at Congo, and gave
them to Jambette who complied. Bouaffesse was visibly impressed by the man's age. The psychologist from Auvergne
hadn't understood that, in such venerable blackmen, the
chief had found, loved, and respected his father (a man
named Gros-Désors for whom he was but number 16).
That's why, before Congo, despite the itching in his cursed
hands, he swayed, pensive. To see this before him: the old
man who takes off his clothes in order to cover the remains
of Solibo, exposing to the sun his mineral skin, his dry
immortal-bamboo body, his flour-sack, not-to-be-found-in-
any-store underpants. His toes were torturing some light
Chinese sandals and clutching the earth. Why stand naked
for a dead corpse, huh Papa? . . . , murmured Bouaffesse,

---

[1] [And if my mama should see this now?! What about respect?!]

craning his neck. Congo threw his arms in the air: *Hé Holibo hilà, wi,* It's Solibo lying here! ... Despite himself, Bouaffesse, turning around, looked at the corpse, but again saw a swollen blackman, a nothing of a blackman like those you run into behind markets, not even tall enough to play basketball, with legs too thin to sow soccer or to ace the hundred-yard dash. And besides, he had died without class, mouth and eyes flung wide open, like a sugarcane cutter struck by a long-one. He came back toward Congo, pen and notebook ready: You say Solibo, but that's not a name, it's some monkey thing. His real name, what is it?

—*Holibo Bidjoul!*

—All right, you don't know his name. And who is it that killed him, huh?

Congo told him about the throat snickt by the word, and Bouaffesse remained mute, suspicious, wondering if he had really heard what he thought he had. With some hesitation he asked him more questions: Huh, Papa, I don't understand how a word can slit someone's throat ... ?

—*Ha di yo di'w!*[1] admitted Congo.

Which in another language can mean: Neither do I!

Disconcerted, Bouaffesse was snacking on his tongue. There was a lot of weird stuff in this case. Not half a liter of answers but a barrel of questions. He seemed so still that Bobé consulted Jambette to find out if the chief had entered a philosophical state, and why doesn't he bash in that old blackman's face there, yeah why? The truth is that the Chief Sergeant was trying to mobilize his resources. The case should have already been turned over to the inspector on duty, in a procedure Bouaffesse did not like at all: it took the

---

[1][What's been said to you's been said to you!]

eventual glory of a photo in the newspapers away from the men in uniform. The inspectors got the meat and left the soaked bread to the police—and without sauce, he always insisted at the union meetings. And since around here, the men of the Department of Criminal Investigation were Frenchmen from France, while those in uniform were native-natal chaps, the transfer of every case came with the gnashing of teeth and the grinding of egos. Things that day were less dramatic: the officer on duty was from here, a learned blackman who had combed the universities before landing in the police force in France, then in the Criminal Brigade of this country. Despite all, the Chief Sergeant was bent on acting on his impulse and solving the problem before calling on him. He owed it to himself to get his brain working on this and find a guilty party in no time. Because *someone had killed someone!* The whole snickting story was the best proof. He saw in the witnesses an incriminating sweat, the pre-confession shifty eyes that betray murderers: however, clutching at each other, the witnesses were all ashiver. That gave him an idea: *conspiracy!* These animals had gotten together to kill the one named Solibo. Ah! the sons of bitches, now they get together to kill a single man, one, two, four, seven, thirteen, plus the stuffed tomato I sent to the hospital, fourteen, fourteen to kill an idiot! They thought they were fighting the Algerian War, geez? This Solibo must have been some chap, Magnificent, they called him Magnificent, but what kind of person was this citizen? . . . Consequently, he was no longer hesitant with Congo. The best way to corner this vicious old blackman was to track him down with French. The French language makes their heads swim, grips their guts, and then they skid like drunks down the pavement. The Chief Sergeant's sixteen years of career policework had roundly shown this technique to be as efficient as blows with a dictionary to the head, balls minced between two chairs, and nasty electric treatments that no doctor (officially) ever divulges.

—Good. Now, Papa, you are going to speak in French for me. I've got to write what you're going to tell me, this is a criminal inquiry now, so no black Negro gibberish, just mathematical French . . . What's your name, huh?

—Onho.

—That, that's your name in the hills. I am asking you for your City Hall Social Security name . . .

—Bateau Français, articulated Congo as if chewing hot conch.

—Tell me in French what's happened to Solibo here . . .

—*Han pa jan halé fwansé.*[1]

—You don't speak French? You never went to school? So you don't even know whether Henry IV ordered "chicken-pot-pie" or "pork-redbeans-and-rice"? . . .

Bystanders flocked around them: *An moun mô,* a dead man! . . . The news rushed down the neighboring streets and set up camp at the end of Jetty Street. Moped cowboys, pirates straying from sails at harbor, taxi drivers, peddlers of knick-knacks for tourists, lug their bodies and curiosities to the scene. Then came the Savanna's gardeners, the employees of the nearby banks, the vendors of iced juice and three-flavored sherbets, some people from the suburbs on the hill, St. Lucians in disguise, semi-invisible Dominicans, two or three rasta early birds, a mad woman covered with white flour, a militant journalist (excited by what could only be a colonialist transgression), and a bushel of those unclassifiable people who somehow still manage (God knows how!)

_____
[1][I never speak French.]

to escape social services. The whole place soon began to re-
semble a market during the sale of red snapper. Screaming.
Astonishment. Sympathies offered to the line of witnesses.
Curses of mysterious origin in the direction of the policemen. Despite the faces Diab-Anba-Feuilles made, the handkerchief that Jambette was exhibiting, and Bobé's regular
tapping on the handle of his weapon, the ambiance was going sour. From the hot day's metal-blue sky the sun was
lengthening the shadows. The Chief Sergeant suddenly realized that he could no longer afford to try anything else to
solve the case. That old man who lied to him with a straight
face despite his old age shook him up. There wasn't any
more time to think of new tricks, Pilon would have to figure
this all out by himself. Congo stood before him, ridiculous
in his underpants, more unfathomable than a Lorraine cliff.

—OK, all right, Papa, Bouaffesse relented, you don't
speak French . . . Tell me exactly what happened to this Mr.
Solibo . . .

Congo told him what he knew. The Chief Sergeant
screwed up his eyes, throwing his head back as old women
do when someone is trying to cheat them. Congo looked
him in the eyes. Pressed for time, Bouaffesse was lost after a
few seconds and put a conciliatory hand on his shoulder:
Papa, I don't get it: when he fell, he yelled *Patat' sa!,* right?

—*Wi!* said Congo.

—When a man yells *Patat' sa,* it's because something's
the matter, no? So, he yells, falls, and no one moves to see
what's going on, to give him some air, a massage with cam-
phor-and-rum, and so you leave him ample time to turn as
stiff as a stale crouton.

—*Wi!* Congo maintains.

So Bouaffesse brandished one of his cursed hands with
more rage than if he was about to smash a long-one to
pieces. But just as he was about to strike, his eyes met those

of the Relic: the graveyard hand remained stuck in the air, trembling with powerlessness, *ab hoste maligno libera nos, domine!*

Congo doesn't move. The malignant hand hovers above his face, but he does not move. We can't see his eyes, only his profile. On the other hand, we get a front view of Ti-Coca: his mustache droops like a folded umbrella. Eyebrows unknotting above hard, round eyes, he deciphers Congo's. Unsettled to see Bouaffesse stopped in his course, Jambette can't stay still. Diab-Anba-Feuilles's tremors set the rhythm at which he advances, ready to slaughter anyone. From our stiff line we watch the confrontation out of the corner of our eyes, so hazardous is it to budge. The onlookers stand a few meters away, sustained in their positions by Bobé, who plays the testy-sheriff-standing-by-a-saloon from the westerns. Without really understanding what's going on, the crowd is aroused by this confrontation between the Chief Sergeant and the old man: Congo should be spared because of his age. Vague comments give way to open threats: It's no good! Hands off the old man! And if it was your father, bastard?! Ti-Coca, leave him alone! . . . Then, intruding from nowhere, reeking of bitterness, comes the supreme insult: *Ti-Coca, b'da manman'w!* . . .[1] Oh, Bouaffesse starts, whistle in his teeth, gun and billyclub in a steel grip. A big shove disperses the onlookers. Diab-Anba-Feuilles stands ready at the side of his chief, ready for any crisis. Taking advantage of the commotion, we start draining away but Jambette threatens us with his murderous handkerchief: Stay here, otherwise there's going to be blood! . . . We get back into the straight line. The Chief Sergeant comes back toward Congo, looking satisfied.

---

[1] [Motherfucker!]

Diab-Anba-Feuilles, hands at his visor, stays behind watching the crowd, etching faces in his memory, storing vendettas. And suddenly, despite the distance between him and them, bakoua hats tilt over eyes, handkerchiefs cover noses. Some simply leave. Relatively calm, Bouaffesse, back near Congo, growls: You almost made me angry, Papa! You really think I'm going to swallow your snickting story?! Solibo falls with a scream of pain and you stand before him like cartoon characters?! Huh?! He already smells like sewage water but no one figured out that he was dead: YOU THINK THE POLICE ARE MICKEY MOUSE OR SOMETHING, GENTLEMEN?! . . . With a spiteful gesture he instructs his men to arrest us. Terror grips us again: No chief, noooo chieeef, we didn't do anything, chieef, enough playing around, chieef, I've got to go to work, oh mama . . . The policemen tame us with slaps and billyclubs, from kicks in the ass to kicks to the head. We fall into the van. The odor reopens old wounds. Piled up around the barred window, we bawl without restraint.

A thousand manioc ants run over Solibo's body. They come out of the earth, the roots, the bark, they come out of the air and out of time, they come from the other end of the world, carriers of a famished eternity beneath which Solibo moves not. It really seems like we have lost the Magnificent. His flesh is living a life that isn't its own. His nylon shirt, his polyester pants, and his little hat are dull. And already, his shoes no longer shine.

Eeeoowiouu eeeoowiioouu the fire-and-rescuemen's trouble began awhile before arriving at the hospital where they were taking Doudou-Ménar. Dazzled by the massive gold of the denture Nono exhibited, they counted their own rotten teeth, and tormented their imaginations with a thousand dental estimates. Thus, Doudou-Ménar opened her eyes among general indifference. The Terrible One leaped so violently from her stretcher that the vehicle staggered, forcing the driver out of the right lane. Where's that bastard? she yelled. Already, swinging Nono-Goldenmaw by his nostrils, she ripped his soft lips and his exposed gums. Flung hard, the policeman broke the back window but by chance remained inside the ambulance. Despite his dismounted jaw, his splashing blood, he threw himself into a desperate search for his dental fortune: *Lô mwen,* my gold! *Lô mwen!* . . . Relieved, the fire-and-rescuemen saw Doudou-Ménar fall back, in a coma. That was but a brief respite, for at the entrance of the hospital emergency ward, they were transferring her onto a gurney when Nono found his mangled denture. The policeman yelled like a fishmonger. His trembling hands picked up the auriferous debris in a handkerchief that he carefully put in his pocket, before he rained blows on the inert mass of the Fat One: *An kè tjwé'y,* I'm going to kill her! . . . That treatment woke up the Terrible One, who made two fire-and-rescuemen, the stretcher, and the gurney fly. She tore off one of the ambulance doors and threw it through the windows of the emergency ward. She picked up Nono-Goldenmaw by the skin of his belly, crumpled him like a sheet of paper announcing the end of welfare payments, and smashed him against the inside walls of the vehicle. The surviving fire-and-rescuemen, nurse-assistants, nurses, stretcher bearers, and the intern on duty, horrified, watched her attempt to leap toward them, before she broke down in a demented burst of laughter and collapsed all at once. The fire-and-rescuemen hurried to add her to the long queue of the Carnival's wounded (these, weeping over their neglected hemorrhages, were wondering what degree of debilitation was necessary to warrant emergent care in this emergency ward), then they recovered

Nono-Goldenmaw, who was no more than a bluish clot, and they laid him too on a gurney in the line. They were just about to go back to their station when the Maniac woke up. Their reflexes were unbelievable. Doudou-Ménar had not even put her foot on the ground when the fire-and-rescuemen drove off in a hurry, siren wailing, flashing lights gone mad. Nono-Goldenmaw, mysteriously aroused from the depths of unconsciousness, flew from his gurney to the stairs nearby. Puzzled by the commotion, the vendor got up, took hold of her gurney, and started to shake up the line of patients. Order in the ward was thus disrupted: a comatose person awoke shaking with a new trauma, another one with barely a scratch suffered a ruptured consciousness and went into a coma, one intern in no rush a minute ago now busied himself over his own blood, and two nurses until then care-free suddenly needed intensive care. At the crest of her frenzy, the Terrible One now made her way toward town and the Savanna, yelling: *Diab-Anba-Fey an ké défolman-té'w,*[1] Diab-Anba-Feuilles, I'm going to kill you! . . . Some passersby seeing her on her way thought she was leading a procession of that carnivalesque day, others thought her the terrible creature of the vidé[2]* of the day before (God! such decadence . . .).

Without seeing the ants, the Chief Sergeant eyed the body scornfully while scratching his behind with both hands. He did that whenever he was at a loss: he had wasted time, got himself in trouble with the fire-and-rescue squad, failed to preserve the scene of the crime in its original state, and knew nothing of the motives for the crime, nor the

---

[1][Diab-Anba-Fey, I'll bend you out of shape!]

[2]A mix of singing and dancing, races and exuberance that concludes our balls. My advice: only engage in such things during Carnival.

identity of the guilty party. His sole consolation: the troop of individuals guarded in the van. His faithful acolytes kept the curious onlookers ten meters away. Only one reporter from the newspaper *France-Antilles* was admitted behind the police line, taking pictures of Bouaffesse and his policemen standing triumphantly over the body, then of the van from which rose prayers and crying. Upon his departure, Bouaffesse went into deep thought near Solibo's body until the onlookers became intolerable and Diab-Anba-Feuilles (convulsing) threatened to silence them. Bouaffesse went back to the van, fingered the radio, growled: Chief Sergeant speaking, put Pilon on the line! . . . , waited by the noisy box, lost patience: You twirling your candycane or what? . . . , and calmed down when the CB poured out an unimpassioned voice: Chief Inspector Pilon here, what's going on? . . . And so the Criminal Brigade took over the death of the Magnificent (bad days come without warning—and I still weep over it).

Chapter 3

Oh friends!

The Chief Inspector

racks his brains

and turns us into the suspects

of a preliminary investigation

(Weep over whom?

Doudou-Ménar.)

By the time the Chief Inspector, Evariste Pilon, got involved in the Solibo affair, the sun had already dissolved the clouds of the night. His shift had gone routinely: reading the current files, writing up reports, outstanding forms. Leaving the usual flow of wounded victims to register their grievances with the Chief Sergeant's office, he had merely come by the station to take care of some formalities. But he had been bored mostly . . . A blackman sporting a goatee and no mustache, always wearing (except in court when he takes oath) an old bakoua hat gone limp from use, Evariste Pilon is a great detective. At least so the newspaper *France-Antilles* crowned him, when in less than a week he solved the case of that quimboiseur who had been poisoned with holy water and when he took care of that appalling mystery of the old mulatto woman found deboned in a sealed hutch. Though a fan of detective novels, the Chief Inspector had never liked the irrational side of "cases" in this country. The initial facts were never reliable, a shadow of unreason, a hint of evil, clouded everything, and despite his long stay in the land of Descartes, since he had been raised in this country like the rest of us with the same knowledge of zombies and various evil soucougnans,* the Inspector's scientific efforts and cold logic often skidded. He stuck to it at the price of rather unpleasant mental exertion, but still dreamed for this country—even on the day of Solibo's death—of a mystery drawn with a compass (and a protractor). Conclusion: he was a policeman with a brain. Not a policeman for moped accidents, stray oxen, Dominicans without papers, petty chicken thieves, or merchants with false scales. Nor one of those cops in dark glasses who shadow anybody who clamors for Independence. A sharp policeman, slyer than a rat without a tail, but who, unfortunately, didn't always find mysteries to stoke his brain in our simple stories of dirty rum and knife fights.

At the time of the Solibo affair, he is living with a freckled chabine, petitions for Creole in the schools but jumps when his children use it to speak to him, crowns Césaire a great poet without ever having read him, venerates the Antilleanity of the July cultural festival with its outdoor theater but dreams of Jean Gosselin's variety shows, commemorates the self-liberation of the slaves and frets at the Schœlcherian masses of the liberating God, disdains the Christmas fir and throws snow on his small Martinican filao tree, observes Frantz Fanon Day, which he considers to be relevant overseas, votes Progressive on the municipal ballot, abstains from the legislative one and screams *Vive de Gaulle!* at the presidential polling places, cultivates a sob for Independence, sets aside one heartbeat for Autonomy and the rest for Martinique being made a *département.** That is to say, he lives like all of us, at two speeds, not knowing whether he should put on the brakes when going uphill or accelerate going down.

One detail: in the shade of his bakoua, under drooping lids which give him a jaded look, Evariste Pilon has the big eyes of a bullfrog tracking maybugs in sugar cane during a drizzle.

He arrived in an unmarked Renault 4L police car. He was followed by a blue Peugeot 403 police station wagon carrying Dr. Siromiel, policemen in civilian clothes with their photographic material, and steel briefcases containing a bunch of bizarre tools. The Chief Sergeant ran up to him:

Hey Inspector, I've done almost all the work for you . . . The Inspector's eyes looked vacant, fatigue dug at his bones, and nervous tics shook the flesh of his cheeks, side effect of the nightly coffee. At the corner of his lips, sprinkling ashes on his goatee, hung a suffocating cigarette butt. His relations with Bouaffesse involved a chemistry of attraction-repulsion: though the colorful fellow was an interesting character, his policework was less so. The Chief Inspector had never actually experienced it, but, from what he gathered from his metropolitan colleagues, investigating with Bouaffesse was like a tropical delirium. His common sense and his reflexes, however, made him useful in some circumstances. Where's the body? grumbled Pilon. They had to penetrate the thick crowd before getting to the area Bouaffesse's acolytes protected. The Chief Inspector waved in greeting and walked toward the tree with measured steps. Slowed down, despite the crowd's furious curiosity, he turned around without looking at the corpse and stared at the ground in fixed surprise. It's nothing, Bouaffesse felt obliged to explain, the fire-and-rescuemen ran around all over the place . . . Pilon, still mute and still astonished, crouched at the fringe of a bloody halo on the ground. It's a suspect's sauce, continued Bouaffesse, she tried to make a circus here, a blow from a billyclub put her back in her place and we sent her to the hospital with Goldenmaw, it's nothing . . . When Pilon worried about so much blood, Bouaffesse said again: Look, it's nothing, she's fat like a big pot of margarine, it will do her some good . . . Her name's Doudou . . . I mean . . . Lolita Boidevan, she's the one who reported the body . . . Then, as if he was waking up, Evariste Pilon pronounced in a clear voice: So the site isn't in its original state. It's been used as a field of battle . . .

—Battle, battle! you're not going to tell me that just because a few blows flew here and there, that World War I was fought here! Which war were you in? If you'd been in Algeria, you'd know what a battle *éti moun ka senyen moun*,[1] where blood really flows, looks like! . . .

The Inspector is not listening to him any more. He barely moves, bends without touching anything, as if trying to soak up the reality. Despite the fear slashing at our insides, we watch him from the van's barred window with the thirst of the open desert before a drop of water. Oh, great is faith: he alone can know and understand that we have nothing to do with it, that Solibo died exclaiming *Patat' sa!*, ejected from life in a twist of fate. Our lamentations roll up and choke us. Charlo' isn't by the window with us: broken down in a corner, he feels with horror his cheek whitened by the accursed slap from which diabolical itches ripple. A flow of sunlight reveals the dust floating in the air, and Sucette hiccups and throws up, weeping at the idea that Solibo's dead, that he's rotting under a tree, without love or respect. Beneath the side window from which you can see the tamarind tree, Ti-Cal, Congo, Bête-Longue, Zozor Alcide-Victor, Pipi, Didon, Zaboca, Cœurillon, and I mingle our shivering and sweat. Sidonise, who had seemed for a few moments to be drowning in another world, starts to murmur an inaudible story. A strange smile transfigures her pain, her eyes follow the flight of internal visions. There is a prowling memory there, of those that death, in its tide, drains from our heads, our hearts, our dreams. Oh life plays hide-and-seek, never giving all of herself at once, but leaving to death's seasons the essence of her stems, her flowers' subtle perfume. There, through the small sherbet vendor, Solibo confronts our distress, dissipates it, as certain

---

[1][Where people make people bleed.]

churches do the sadness of the devoted. Charlo' forgets his cheek and raises his inundated eyes.

He was there when I bought the shark, Sidonise murmurs. Not one of those sharks that eat people, but a good nurse shark, smooth, with pink flesh. I hadn't seen him in a long while, and without him I lived like a bird fallen from the nest, with ruffled feathers and thwarted sleep. With Dalta, things hadn't gone very far, and I was alone again with the children. Dalta had left, saying my heart was too full of something for someone else, that though he knocked at the door, no one came to open. I hadn't said anything to Dalta, because he was right. Solibo lived everywhere in me, they say in the heart, but I think he lived in my belly too, he lived in my dreams, and in my memory he had wrecked everything, you know, like a cursed fig tree, murdering its surroundings. How to name this? If something amused me, I was down because he wasn't there to laugh with me. When the afternoon was pretty, no child was sick, the garden was generous, the sherbet sold better than salted meat, when in me life rose lighting up my eyes, bringing songs to my lips, it made me sick that Solibo wasn't there to live those moments with me. So I would comb out my sadness, do her hair in different ways, pour the water of my youth into her as one does with those plants which are sparing with their flowers. What do you call this? (We don't know, Sidonise, we don't know . . .) That's not all, I didn't have the courage to go before him like a bunch of picked flowers, to tell him: Look, Solibo, your woman is pining away . . . I am like that, my braids aren't braids, but vines of pride and when my heart chokes, when I feel like I'm drowning, it's pride that I live, that I eat, that I breathe, like those cars that ran on alcohol during the war. But I liked to go hear his words, without him seeing me, and since I never knew where he was going to talk, I asked around, here and there, offering a sherbet to whoever knew where I could listen to Solibo. Ah! Sucette, you got sherbet after sherbet from me that way! (But your sherbets are good, Sidonise . . .) So when I saw him near the boat where I buy my shark, I told him: Solibo, get out of my way so I can go cook my stew . . . Heh, heh, it was a way of telling him: *Solibo, come taste Sidonise's sharkstew* . . . He had understood me since I hadn't even put down my bag when he rolled down to my house. Yes, I was happy! He was the one who cut off the shark's head, gutted it, and scalded it to skin it. With the gestures of an officiating priest, he placed the pieces of fish in the marinade pan. He tried to make me giddy with his words, but I smelled his scent, I rubbed my shoulder against his shoulder, I looked at him sideways, happy as a dragonfly under the dew. I must say I also watched the work of his hands, because Solibo is good with food! When he made you a casserole or a real z'habitant* soup, you had to be careful not to bite your fingers, your mouth drooled so much! (Oh, beautiful words, Sidonise . . .) I spied on his marinade with piercing eyes, I counted the lemons he pressed, the pinches of salt, his way of crushing the hot red pepper and of cutting the green one, of pounding the pepper, garlic cloves, and oil before stirring them in. But after the onions and the warm water, when a blessed perfume made the fish sing, I understood that Solibo had had me once again: his marinade was still his secret! (Yeah, he was tricky, Sidonise . . .) Then he washed the rice, longer than you would wash your underwear, put it on the fire, washed it again after the first boiling the way the people from Réunion do. There, I stopped looking, because not a soul can teach Sidonise how to handle rice! I listened to him babble while I was sweetening a madou* for the punch. Then we sipped, exchanging nothings, I told him that Dalta had left, that I was alone, but he only watched for the rice's steam, the work of the marinade which he stirred without stopping. Maria, do you smell that, Maria? . . . The shark's flesh breathed out spices, smells of seashells were rising. Our noses were open to all of them and we let ourselves drool . . . Maria, my dear, close the window or your neighbors are going to show up, laughed Solibo. He was right. Some gourmet-mouth men had already started to prowl: *Hello there, Ma'am Sidonise, how are the children?* . . . and sniff-sniff here . . . sniff-sniff there . . . *So Ma'am Sidonise, I haven't seen you in a while, you're doing all right?* . . . , and they stretched their necks sniff-sniff . . . , sniff-sniff . . . I closed one eye and I looked at them sideways: So, such-and-such, last night did you dream you'd run into me today?! . . . Solibo shook me out of the way and invited them to come in. A little while later, twelve drooling mouths were crowding my kitchen, drying out my rum bottle, and looking at the shark in my pan with pain in their eyes. You wouldn't believe how nice they were to me all the sudden! *Sidonise, I'm going to come repair the rusty sheet on your roof . . . Sidonise, how come you never call me to cart away that gas tank of yours, it's going to come down on your head!* . . . et cetera. Finally, the time came when the shark in the marinade smelled right. The rice had been cooked for a long while. I had rinsed it and was letting it drain. So Solibo began the stewing. Of course none of those gourmet-mouth blackmen had taken off. They hung around with all of that *But Ma'am Sidonise, tell us how so-and-so is doing . . . So, tell about your godchild's health?* . . . et cetera et cetera. Good God (Yeah, Sidonise, tell it, tell us the tale), when Solibo sautéed the yellow hot pepper, the French onion, the garden spices in the oil, the drooling mouths trembled! When he dropped in the five tomatoes, the garlic, when he had ground the parsley, and sprinkled the pepper-salt, the waiting mouths became all gray with dry saliva. Solibo pretended not to see their colossal greed, and slowed down his movements, looking only at his hands under the porch of his eyes. I looked as serious as on the day of my communion, but in my heart I was laughing, like I was a hunchback with no mirror around. Those ravenous ones could have choked, you know, when Solibo made the pieces of shark sweat before letting them drop in the pot full of golden spices! Imagine the shark sinking in the hot oil and cooking in the perfume and the colors of the fried spices (We are, Sidonise, we are). Oh la la la la, even I sat around with drooling mouth and drifting eyes, just like the rest of them. Solibo was taking his sweet little time, doing things with his pinky lifted in the air: Vinegar if-you-pleeze, and three cloves thank-you-much, juice from a lemon not too young and not too old if-you-pleeze . . . I obeyed as if I were a high-waist quadrille dancer at the Ball of the Wise. The avid ones had closed my shutters and doors as shields against more newcomers. So, ha, ha, ha, we gathered around in the dark around the stewpot, like a gang of thieves around a béké's wallet. The children got back from school just on time, and we ate the shark, the sauce, the bones, the rice, we scoured the stewpot and polished the bowls, and then we also sucked on the wine and all remaining rum bottles. The voracious neighbors had left with pregnant women's bellies, walking like ducks. That's when Solibo said: *Maria, darling, I hadn't forgotten you, no . . .*

A sob submerges her voice, but the Magnificent floats in the dust of the van, with gleams that he steals from the sun. As he retreats and Sidonise seems to withdraw into herself, we flock back to the barred window, brought back to the misfortune . . . Outside, calm has returned to the crowd. Wearing hat and tie, the Chief Inspector captivates everyone with his gestures of a hunter in an invisible forest.

The silence is now complete. Diab-Anba-Feuilles's tremors have almost ceased. Bobé still drools but no longer acts as if he were a deputy. Dr. Siromiel and the other inspectors wait in a circle. Their good-students' eyes tell us that every one of Pilon's movements around Solibo is in accordance with an exact science.

After a few minutes of reflection, the Chief Inspector beckoned to Dr. Siromiel. Together they approached Solibo's body. Pilon always calls on this same doctor whenever a gruesome discovery falls into his purview. He's stocky, round, slower than the town of Prêcheur when the sun is high. While Bouaffesse flung away Congo's rags, they examined the body silently. Bouaffesse rolled up the clothes and stuffed them under his arm and stood back. Evariste Pilon sighed and, turning toward him, said: You touched the body? . . . What do you take me for, a rookie? Bouaffesse became indignant. You see him now just as his misery made him! . . . Pilon, not at all insistent, just wanted to know the facts, and Bouaffesse recited what he knew of the one named Solibo who bullshits stories, who yells *Patat' sa!,* falls boom! without anyone during all that time thinking of getting off their ass to go see what happened, since the body was stiff when I came.

—Very stiff or just a bit?

—Pardon me?

—Only stiff at the joints or completely stiff? Dr. Siromiel intervened.

—That's a philosophical question or what?

—Was the body hot, warm, or cold? Evariste Pilon went on.

Bouaffesse said that the body was icy like a vanilla sherbet, that there were thirteen witnesses in the van, excluding the stuffed tomato who was at the hospital, and that they were all shivering like murderers, which wasn't surprising since it was evident that the corpse didn't die of old age after collecting his social security, and like mathematics teaches us: a murdered body without a scratch equals poison . . . But neither the Chief Inspector nor the doctor was listening to these insights any more: crouching, they scrutinized Solibo. The Chief Sergeant walked away, disgusted.

Pilon and Siromiel spoke in a whisper.

—They must have tried to help him: the belt is loose . . .

—No wound?

—No blood, in any case . . .

—So, what do you think it was?

—What?

—Cause of death?

—Asphyxiation.

—You sure?

—It's probable: his lips are cyanotic. Look at the color of the nails.

They came even closer to the body. Pilon was careful not to touch it. On the other hand, Siromiel tried to move Solibo's limbs, felt his abdomen, his cheeks, and was spitting out his findings: cadaverous odor is clearly perceptible—rigidity very pronounced—no ecchymosis—pupils are round—no subcutaneous hemorrhaging—death occurred more than four hours ago . . .

—Positive?

—Positive.

Siromiel continued the examination in silence, palpating the skull, inspecting the open mouth, feeling the neck, the groin, slipping his hand under the body to explore its back. A few minutes later he got up, more somber than a spider at the approach of rain: This man was in perfect health . . .

—He died a healthy man?—Pilon tried his hand at irony.

—Correct. The death was accidental.

—Anything else?

—I confirm asphyxiation.

—Which would have happened how?

—An autopsy would tell . . . There's some blood-streaked mucus in the mouth . . .

—So?

—Suspicious death.

It was as if Dr. Siromiel had pronounced "Open Sesame." Pilon straightened up, and his heart started to race to the rhythm of the great hunt: Stand aside for a little while, Doctor . . .

Obeying Pilon's signal, an inspector approaches and starts taking pictures. At that point, though the camera isn't even pointed in their direction, some fools run away, others turn around, even we, in the van, get away from the window: no one has happy memories from police Kodak moments. But the terrible photographer is only interested in the body and the debris that surrounds it. Led by Pilon's cabalistic signs, he takes pictures of the whole place, then of Doudou-Ménar's blood, Sucette's drum, our demijohn, the crushed tamarinds, the empty potato crates, and the rocks which served as our stools, he takes pictures of this, he takes pictures of that, a small bottle, bat crap, Solibo from above, Solibo from below, Solibo from the sides, click and click, he takes pictures of the etcetera, the Amen, and the Hail Mary, and when he's done taking pictures, well my friends, proof that he isn't paying for the film, he takes more pictures. Pilon during that time sends out his other inspectors. They come and go with long and short rulers. They handle brushes and strange powders, they crouch and collect some footprints on special paper, make plaster casts, some drawings, pick through the dust, use tweezers to put some rubbish into labeled plastic bags. Pilon is at the center of the dance: he blackens Solibo's fingers with ink and presses them on a piece of paper, and empties the corpse's pockets. The demijohn and the drum are wrapped as if they were relics of the Madonna, sealed, and then taken to the station wagon. Now, they cover certain places with wax paper. All this appears so diabolical that, fingers crossed, we murmur the Our Father: in these ill-fated times, a blackman's prayer is never useless . . .

Toward the end of the bustling of the Office of Criminal Records, Pilon rejoined the Chief Sergeant who was trying to scare the crowd away with his dirty looks: Siromiel says that the death is suspicious . . . Bouaffesse sneered and said you didn't need to be a rocket scientist to figure that out . . . It's poison, I told you that from the beginning . . .

—Siromiel did not conclude that . . .

—He doesn't have the eye . . . He's already tired . . .

—Show me the witnesses . . .

That's when a roar froze everyone in their tracks, when a bleeding Doudou-Ménar flew out of the crowd screaming: *Diab-Anba-Fey an ké défolmanté'w,* Devil, I'm going to kill you!

The Big Bag fell on Diab-Anba-Feuilles as powerfully as the heat comes down on the market's sheet-iron roof in Carême. Without further ado, she set off a blast of slapping and twenty-two blows to his head. The crowd broke into blackbird screams, trampling Jambette and Bobé who dashed forward to the rescue. Doudou-Ménar was massacring her prey with the rage of a mounted gendarme during an agricultural strike. Pilon and a few others vainly tried to push back the drifting crowd. Giving some malicious blows here and there, Bouaffesse blazed himself a trail. Reaching the Tigress, he smashed the bloody bandage that crowned her head. The Terrible One roared, left Diab-Anba-Feuilles, and charged energetically at the already sensitive liver of the Chief Sergeant, who howled a solo of agony but succeeded in catching the enraged woman between his cursed hands. Doudou-Ménar felt the dissipation of her vital warmth. A sudden coldness froze her beneath the billyclubs of Jambette and Bobé, who had been rescued from the crowd. Thirteen kinds of unkindness fell on the unfortunate woman before Pilon and a few other inspectors were able to intervene. When Jambette and Bobé were overpowered and Bouaffesse's grip was finally unclenched, Doudou-Ménar irreparably collapsed over Diab-Anba-Feuilles's epileptic jolts—and the crowd's panic doubled.

(Solibo Magnificent used to tell me: "Oh, Oiseau, you want Independence, but that idea weighs you down like handcuffs. First, be free before the idea. Then: make a list of the things in your head and in your stomach that chain you up. That's where it starts, that struggle of yours . . .")

The Chief Sergeant has taken control of the situation: he has calmed the crowd with two Hey-there's, posted Jambette and Bobé to contain it, and called for reinforcements by radio. A new ambulance has arrived. Informed of the misadventures of their colleagues, these fire-and-rescuemen stay under cover, evidently worried about the reasons for the call. The Chief Sergeant shows them his gums, which might mean: don't move! . . . Right there and then, three police vans spill onto the path in a bluish multitude. Blazing with anticipatory rage, the new policemen charge the open crowd, overpowering a few guys with shifty eyes—just in case. Bouaffesse calms them with one hand. Don't get excited, pleeze! . . . Where are the barricades I asked for? . . . Without a word, the troops return to the vans and bring back the barricades with which they cordon off the tamarind tree. Jambette and Bobé appear to be in disguise amidst the impeccable uniforms of the new policemen who roll bewildered eyes at the inanimate body of Diab-Anba-Feuilles. Bouaffesse posts them along the barricades in an impressive line. The crowd slowly returns, three times thicker. This time the number of policemen incites the mob to church silence. Picking up their material and plastic bags, the inspectors from the Criminal Records Office leave, putting pedal to the metal. The Chief Sergeant nervously wipes his shining face: What, what, what, what the . . . ! he sputters at Pilon and Dr. Siromiel who are crouched near Doudou-Ménar, my man's lying here on the ground like a pregnant woman with heatstroke, and you, you're taking care of the woman who premeditated willful assault and battery of a policeman and with no extenuating circumstances?! I mean, you racist or what?! . . . The Chief Inspector looks bored. Siromiel, bent over Doudou-Ménar, vigorously massages her heart: Fire-and-rescue, quick! he gasps. Bouaffesse pretends not to hear and conspicuously kneels next to Diab-Anba-Feuilles. Evariste Pilon straightens up and beckons them with emphatic gestures; they answer with an anxious twisting of fingers. It's obvious that they don't want to risk entering this police mangrove. The

Chief Inspector rushes over with such determination that they leap out of the ambulance: Hey, look here, we didn't do anything, we've got nothing to do with this ... *Hurry! Cardiac arrest,* spits Pilon. Flwap! Fears forgotten, the fire-and-rescuemen seize their oxygen bottles, their tubes, their red-crossed cases, their stretcher, and hurry.

Their nervousness was now thickening over the body of the Fat One: Siromiel was testing her pupils with a penlight, tracking a pulse in her throat, her groin, her wrists, one fire-and-rescueman was giving her oxygen, another was massaging her heart with an energy that would break marble. All acted with anxious haste and precision. Turning his back to them, the Chief Sergeant pompously greeted Diab-Anba-Feuilles, who was staggering to his feet. Soon, Dr. Siromiel dried his hands on his handkerchief and, avoiding Pilon's interrogating eyes, left Doudou-Ménar's body for Solibo's. What are you lookin' for? said Pilon, joining him. This death puzzled the doctor, a disagreeable feeling. Poisoning was possible, but there was no froth in the mouth, no pupil dilatation, not even a significant change in the complexion. The cyanosis could be due to a lung edema following an ingestion of barbiturates, but that hypothesis, along with the others, could only be confirmed by an autopsy. Pilon suggesting internal hemorrhage provoked by the possible swallowing of ground bamboo, the doctor protested saying that there wasn't the characteristic paleness here. There's also the milk of the manchineel tree, continued Pilon, caught up in his review of the poisons of the country.

— Such sap irritates the lips, said the doctor, his are clean ... These ants are strange ... Still, I don't think it's poisoning ...

— So you don't know for sure?

— One thing. The woman, the Fat One . . .

—What about her?

— She's dead.

MOTHERCROCKER! exclaims Bouaffesse, shoving aside
the frightened fire-and-rescuemen. He lifts the blanket
from Doudou-Ménar's remains, incredulous: Did you really
make sure it's not some wicked fainting spell? I bet she's just
putting on some kind of show . . . He grabs the unfortunate
woman under her arms, lifts her up, pats her cheeks: Lolita,
Lolita, it's Philémon . . . His face is dripping, new haloes
darken the blue of his shirt under his arms. The fire-and-
rescueman, sheltered by their oxygen bottles, watch his
efforts. Jambette and Bobé have come nearer, ready. Wild-
eyed, Diab-Anba-Feuilles stands aside. Pilon gets Bouaffesse up and says: Have the ambulance carry the body to the
hospital morgue, and dispatch someone to her residence to
inform her family. Also, tell the fire-and-rescuemen to pick
up this . . . , by the way, who is that man? He doesn't have
any papers on him . . . Solibo Magnificent? No one knows
his real name? Not even the witnesses? OK, so get the body
to Dr. Lélonette, I'll get an autopsy order from the District
Attorney . . . Then we'll see the witnesses . . . This woman
was one of them, no?

—Yes. Lolita Boidevan, called Doudou-Ménar.

—Why this raging aggression against your officer?
Anything to do with the case . . .

—Not even remotely! That crazy woman was insane
in the brain! . . .

The fire-and-rescuemen loaded Doudou-Ménar's body,
then turned their attention to Solibo's. The Chief Inspector was talking into his radio. Siromiel, eyes closed, proba-

bly falling asleep, sat in the back of the unmarked police car. Most of the policemen had gone back into the vans, a few scrupulous ones still attempted to disperse the crowd. Diab-Anba-Feuilles, Jambette, and Bobé, having sought shelter in their vehicle, waited for the sign to move off, but Bouaffesse was keeping his eye on the fire-and-rescuemen, who were having difficulties. Astride over the Magnificent's body, they had taken hold of him, but despite their heave-ho's! they couldn't lift him off the ground: Solibo weighed a ton all the sudden, like the corpses of those blackmen unwilling to leave this life. Doesn't want to leave, chief, they quavered, he's heavier than the Robert Factory, if we lift him we'll bust our balls . . . With one short whistle, Bouaffesse got Jambette, Diab-Anba-Feuilles, and Bobé to help. But Solibo weighed a ton and a half. He called the two men guarding the barricade. But Solibo weighed two tons. He rounded up the men from one of the vans: the policemen piled up over the body, fighting for a grip. But Solibo weighed five tons. The men of Law started to knead their blessed crucifixes, their usual quimbois amulets concealed under their shirts. Even the Chief Sergeant was silent. Everyone knew that the dead could start to gain weight, they had seen hearses spin out of control right near the cemetery, but none of them had ever confronted such a phenomenon with their own muscles. Diab-Anba-Feuilles, who claimed to be born with a caul (and therefore protected from all evil spells), gave the instructions: First, the feet, pull in zigzags, good, recite Our Father and pull to the left, good, let's see, who didn't get baptized? Those who didn't get baptized should take thirteen steps back and cross their fingers. One, two, three: Saint Michael! . . . Well, um, we're going to imagine it's a yam. Ready? let's go . . . Good, who's got holy water? . . . The arrival of the Chief Inspector interrupted their oys and, contributing to the vain efforts until he was dead with fatigue, Evariste Pilon, drop-jawed, rediscovered (in situ) one of our local mysteries.

(Without wanting to bore you, one word: the proper burial of the dead has been lost. These days, they carry him like a sack of guano in padded coffins designed for countries with winters. One must, on the other hand, respectfully untie the threads the departed one keeps on this life. Without crying over tradition, let's remind ourselves: four shoulders, at an hour of the rising sun, a certain way of walking when going down, a rhythm when going up, a swaying of the hips over the ravines, a line that turns and coils, that sometimes retreats into a reinvented landscape. Through the sheet, the deceased would feel the pain of his friends, hear their heartbeat, drink their sweat.)

The crowd was coming and going round. The curious ones bent over the barricade, studying the anxious attention the police devoted to the body: What, *sakini?*[1] They can't lift it? ... The Chief Sergeant scratched his ass. Pilon looked at Solibo with insomniac eyes, staring as if he had seen a horse with three hoofs. Diab-Anba-Feuilles and a few other stubborn ones were still sweating and exhausting themselves over the body, while still others, including the fire-and-rescuemen, stood aside, ready for a strategic withdrawal. Coming to from his nap, eyes barely open, Dr. Siromiel reminded them about the existence of his office, his numerous patients, and how late he was. Thirty years of dealing with

---

[1][Whatsgoinon?]

death in our wonderland had anesthetized his emotional capacities, so much so that when Pilon told him of the impossibility of moving the body, the old man cut him short flwap! Well, get a crane! . . . The policemen, full of respectful astonishment, watched him slump like a hunting dog into the Renault 4L and peacefully fall asleep. While the Chief Sergeant dragged his feet toward the radio in the van, Evariste Pilon who was following him caught sight of our lunar eyes through a reflection in the barred window. He took the time to listen to what Bouaffesse stammered into the radio (Yeah . . . the crane . . . some stuff to lift here . . . why you asking me this bushel of questions? Your name, what is it? mine is the Chief, send the tow crane, and *é fouté mwen lapé!*[2] yes, in the Savanna . . .), then opened the back door. That's where the Inspector saw us and we him from up close for the first time.

Pilon had barely unlocked the door when Sidonise and Conchita leapt up. They had been watching the handle for a long time. Pilon gave a start. They could have easily gotten out had Bouaffesse not sprung up, seizing Conchita's hair and clutching the skin on Sidonise's hips: Where is it you ladies are going, huh? Sidonise grimaced: the cursed hand chilled her skin through the cotton of her dress, and Conchita knelt under the threat of getting a broken neck. Hey where do you think you're going? . . . Bouaffesse was like a hot pepper, his eyes glowed red like the best charcoal, the two women's moaning slaked deep-seated thirsts. Pilon intervened, and the Chief Sergeant, reluctantly letting them go, yelled a *Get back in!* which sent them back to us again, unharmed but shaken from the contact with the mortuary hands. Ti-Cal and Zaboca helped them sit down. *A typical*

---

[2][Get out of my hair! (a standard French expression translated into Creole).]

escape attempt! thundered Bouaffesse in the direction of Pilon, I told you those people weren't clean, didn't I! The Chief Inspector stared at us, looking hard at our hands, our clothes, our shoes. He also tried to make eye contact, but it was difficult. Ladies and gentlemen, he finally uttered, I am from the Department of Criminal Investigation. This is Chief Sergeant Philémon Bouaffesse. Per Articles 76, 77, and 78 of the Code of Penal Procedure, you are in custody for the purposes of a preliminary inquiry. There's no reason you should be worried. It's routine procedure . . . He waited vainly for some reaction, we were piled up in the corner farthest from the door, frightened by Ti-Coca's presence. Pilon, noticing some strong effluvium, inquired about it of Bouaffesse, who took delight in telling him that we had sucked on the demijohn while Solibo was dying. So it contained alcohol, Pilon reacted, then had Siromiel roused from his catnap to perform the procedure referred to by Articles L99, R14, in accordance with the code for alcohol consumption and measures for the prevention of alcoholism . . . Sweet Jesus! whistled Bouaffesse, a lot more impressed than we were—a lot more.

Flanked by policemen, each witness was brought to the car where Dr. Siromiel examined his pupils, smelled his breath, and asked him to open his arms and to hop on one foot. Which task, except for Sidonise and Conchita, invariably threw them on the ground. *A, zot sousé y'neg,*[1] you savored it! exclaimed Bouaffesse. The new policemen gone, only two guards by the barricade contained the movement of a crowd now much thinner. The falling witnesses still succeeded in provoking a few jeers. *Wasta! Basta'd!* . . . But the town fair atmosphere had faded. Diab-Anba-Feuilles

---

[1][Ah, you did some sucking, blackman!]

guarded the van's doors, Jambette and Bobé escorted the witnesses' every step, for blood tests, a hearing with the Chief Inspector sitting in the car, notebook on his lap. The Chief Sergeant, surrounded by the fire-and-rescuemen who ate up his jokes, stood by the door, mean and taunting.

—Full legal name, nickname, profession, age, permanent address?

—Huh?

—Tell us how they call you, explains Bouaffesse.

—Bête-Longue.

—Is that a nickname? Good. What's your full legal name?

—Huh?

—What did your mother tell the Town Council she called you, Bouaffesse translates.

—*An pa save* . . .

—He says he doesn't know, Inspector . . .

—Thank you, Chief Sergeant, but I understand Creole.

—Just trying to be helpful! You're an inspector, you shouldn't delve into the patois of these bums.

—It's a language, Chief Sergeant.

—Where did you read that?

— . . .

—Well then, if it's a language, how come your tongue is always rolling off such a polished French? And why don't you write your report in it?

—That's not the issue, Evariste Pilon interrupts. We'll have to find out this man's civil status. Mr. Longue-Bête, what is your age, profession, and permanent address?

—Huh?

—The Inspector asks you what hurricane you were

born after, what you do for the béké, and what side of town you sleep at night? Bouaffesse specifies.

—I was born right before Admiral Robert, I fish with Kokomerlo on Rive-Droite, and I stay at Texaco, by the fountain . . .

—Tell us what transpired.

—Huh?

—What happened to Solibo? Bouaffesse transmits.

—*Pawol la bay an gôjet,* the word slit his throat . . .

With every opening of the door, we were bathed in a tide of sunlight. One of us then had to get up, coast from window to window onto the abyss of a step which Diab-Anba-Feuilles delighted in watching our efforts to avoid falling from. Whoever came back to the van suffered an inquisitive welcome: hands grabbed him, envious that he was done, anxious to hear his mishaps: What did they do to you? Did Ti-Coca touch you? . . . Our questions summoned no answers, and the ghost listened to them, folded in a corner, in mute beatitude. Then turning back to the barred window whose filthiness soured the flood of light, we let our eyes follow the next one being taken, his acrobatics in front of Siromiel, his at-attention before Pilon, his pain at not being released, instead having to rejoin us. Then, right before the door's luminous rush, we'd glance at Solibo Magnificent, wrecked in a storm of roots, with bitterness and our share of sadness in our eyes.

All the statements were the same: Solibo Magnificent who speaks, speaks, speaks, who collapses screaming *Patat' sa!,* the company who waits, who sucks on the demijohn, listening to Sucette's drum, then Congo who gets up, et cetera . . .

—And how long did you sit there listening to his solo?

All the statements were the same: What is time, Mr. Inspector? . . . Evariste Pilon remained indifferent to that question. For him, time was seconds, minutes, hours, he waved his watch, showing its hands to the witnesses, demanding an answer, even if approximate. Chamzibié, word scratcher, threw senseless questions back at him: How to know time that goes by, Mr. Inspector? Time is grains of rice? A roll of cloth measured with the ruler the way the Syrians do? Where does it go through when it goes by: through the front or the back door? Solibo slid into the roots, so we just waited, like in this country, everywhere, people wait. What's yesterday and what's tomorrow when you wait? . . . He also said that the philosophers had already settled that question. —Ti-Cal took refuge in abstruse politics. Which time? No really, which time? With neither Autonomy nor Independence, there's only tempest or dead time . . . —At the markets, said Pipi and Didon, the job no longer set the pace of life, the carts no longer creaked. So what is time? —There's no longer any place to let the drum ring, wept Sucette, its voice no longer hails day or night, and I, to make it worse, am even more dumb, so what is time?—For music, *there isn't any,* simply stated Charlo' who, without his disappeared orchestra, had less sense in him than a moth lost at noon. —Richard Cœurillon and Zaboca spoke of a time of harvests and smokestack factories, at that time one man handled a machine, the other a scythe, that was time, but now if the fields are deserted and the factory whistles no longer give rhythm to the day, now that your hands no longer know how to lash a rope, braid, nail, cut anything, where does time happen, Inspekder? Some say it's in France, that there,

there is time. —Congo creolized about a manioc time, about the time people actually ate it around here, when he could see the plant grow and count its seasons, but today, all he knew about time was the planes taking off over his hutch into the airport sky.—As for Sidonise, there was once a time when her sherbet maker told her the time, time to flavor the milk with coconut, time to turn the crank in the ice and salt, but today the sherbet was made elsewhere, she bought it in plastic boxes and put it in her sherbet maker for style, since then she glided over the hours and everything else. —Bête-Longue understood nothing of the question, he didn't even know his name, or his birthplace, and nothing either of how many years there were in a day. —Conchita no longer lived under the sun, she only lived at night; her only landmarks were the shadowy flights on a fickle moon. —Zozor Alcide-Victor, finally, had never had an important enough position in his store, which was run by a manager, to learn how to evaluate time, please accept my deepest apologies Inspector . . . As the Chief Inspector, refuting such logic, now considered a possible conspiracy, the Chief Sergeant became more receptive: Could be they aren't completely wrong. When I was unemployed after Algeria, and I sometimes found myself by a ka-drum, ten thousand years could go by and you could have even cut my balls I wouldn't have moved, you know! And then if there was a demijohn of tafia going round . . .

—I beg you, Chief Sergeant, let's not get everything mixed up! . . .

—*The storyteller suddenly stops speaking and this unexpected silence doesn't worry you?*

All the statements were the same: silence is speech. And we even waited tranquilly, because from the word you build the village, but from silence you construct the world. What's more, there's as much silence in speech as there is speech in silence. Who fears silence around here? Silence rings and resounds and means as much as a voice. It's a question of ear, Inspector, the storyteller's speech is the sound from his throat, but it's also his sweat, the rolling of his eyes, his belly, the gestures he draws with his hands, his smell, that of his listeners, the sound of the ka-drum, and all the silences. Plus, you have to add the night, the rain if it rains, and the world's silent vibrations. Who fears silence around here? No one fears silence, especially not one of Solibo's . . . Incredible! said Pilon, infuriated, after each witness, this doesn't make any sense! This apology for silence comes at the right time to accommodate everyone! They agreed on the answers together, Chief Sergeant, we have here a conspiracy to commit murder . . .

—Mr. Bête-Longue . . .

—Huh?

—What happened when Mr. Congo realized that Solibo was dead?

—We rubbed his body right away to warm his blood . . .

—That was when you removed his shoes, unbuttoned his shirt, loosened his belt . . .

—Huh?

—He asks if you messed with his clothes? Bouaffesse completes.

—We rubbed him, dammit!

—He says: yes.

—I understood him, Chief Sergeant . . . How much time went by between your interventions and the time when Mrs. Boidevan went to look for a doctor?

—Huh?

—Chief Sergeant, explain the question to him . . .

—The Inspector asks you if you gave out many a useless word before Doudou-Ménar came down to get me?

—*Yonn dé* . . .[1]

—He says: Not long . . .

—A minute, two minutes, an hour?

—Huh?

—See here, Inspector, translate for yourself, says Bouaffesse, discouraged before such delicate notions.

That first round of questioning completed, Siromiel needed a ride back to his office. Evariste Pilon picked Bobé. Quite pleased with himself, the latter listened with papal gravity to the explanations concerning the blood sample, the medical exam forms to relay to various experts. Afterward, Bouaffesse specified, you're going to park the béké's car at the station and then you go home . . . So it's at this point that Bobé left the Solibo case—since then he's doing very well thank you.

The witnesses were once again locked up in the van. Glued to the ambulance transistor, the fire-and-rescuemen were betting on the hit parade: the agony that "Shleu-Shleu" could supplant "Perfecta" translated into nervous sucking on dead cigarette butts. Diab-Anba-Feuilles had fallen asleep standing against one of the van doors. He didn't snore, but his wide-open mouth kneaded thick breaths. Jambette, resting his elbows on the wheel, picked at his warts, squinting in the rear-view mirror. The usual 86 degrees were there, born of a vertical sun which nearly erased the shadows. The alizé diffused Solibo's fumes, arousing the curiosity of an undiminishable remainder of onlookers. Only some leftover

---

[1][lit., "One two"; "a few . . ."]

blackmen forgotten by life were still poking by the barricade: *Saki tué'y*,[1] who killed him? . . . The Chief Sergeant had rejoined the Chief Inspector, sheltered under a tamarind tree, outside of Solibo's sequestered perimeter. If the crane doesn't get here right away, sighs Bouaffesse, the body will be rotten before the hour, and eaten by ants . . . These mad ants are strange, aren't they? asked Pilon. With his crumpled jacket nestled under his arm, he had loosened his tie and was using his hat as a fan, baring his balding head. Bouaffesse attracted the flies, they twirled their dances in his face. He took the time to stop one on his mustache, to count its feet, before scientifically explaining that they were manioc ants and not mad ants, that there were four ant species, the biting, the black, the mad, and the manioc, that in the manioc kind, there was a difference between the itty-bitty holy-day herbivores, the brick-red ones which navigated underground, and the winged winter messengers. All were gathered on Solibo, he specified. He had barely articulated that thought when he realized the strangeness of what he had just said: *Good God! the manioc ant only lives in Guadeloupe!* . . . Crazed, he sprung over the barricade in the direction of Solibo, sowing cops in his wake who (without understanding what was up, but you never know) gripped their clubs. *A-ah! Sé fonmi manyoc kila wi,* Those really are manioc ants! he screamed for an alarmed Pilon to hear. Anxious to confirm this enigma, he solicited the input of a sleepwalking Diab-Anba-Feuilles who grumbled: If we were in Guadeloupe, I'd say to you manioc ants, chief . . .

—We're in Martinique here, so what do you say?

Diab-Anba-Feuilles took off his cumbersome cap to better examine the astonishing multitude ferreting about

---

[1] [What killed him?]

the Magnificent's body, breathing a formic life into it. All Solibo's energy seemed to have invaded his epidermis, gripped by a siege psychosis. The ants didn't feed themselves, they simply followed the lines of strength around the eyes, along the neck, near the heart, and around the lower belly, in an obscure choreography of homage. Jambette came to contribute his mute surprise to the incredulous silence in which the little group remained stranded, but tracked down by an impatient Bouaffesse: So, what do you see here? . . . , he murmured with great prudence: It looks like, um, ants disguised as manioc ants, chief . . .

Dripping despite the tamarind's shadow and the zephyrs under his bakoua, Pilon resisted this new mystery. From Bouaffesse's excitement (*Manioc ants in Martinique!*) which set off alarm bells for the entomological science of Father Pinchon—not to mention a squall of other suppositions—Pilon diverged onto a long theory on this crime which he now judged undeniable. It was abnormal that the listeners to the one named Solibo manifested no surprise when, having collapsed after a cry of pain, he interrupted his statements in a necessarily illogical way. This permits the hypothesis that the listeners *knew* that the man was going to die and that *they came to observe the spectacle.* This allows us to surmise that all of them, to different extents, had good reason to hold something against this man. These reasons should be ferreted out during the twenty-four-hour custody. He added: We'll have to corner the drum player, the one called Sucette, the only one who's been sufficiently near the victim to realize (if he was telling the truth) that the latter was in agony: it will be hard for him to maintain his original statement . . . Anxious not to be left out of the remaining revelations, Bouaffesse now geared up, suggesting that they should also put the squeeze on the only fellow who got up, probably the group's expert, who would know the exact time when Solibo died since he had provided the poison, as his sorcerous look and his negrified name Congo certainly attested . . . Here's the winch, said Evariste Pilon, reverting to more sober thoughts.

The towtruck came down the alley and parked in front of the memorial. The driver, an albino with dark glasses and a fat cigar, waited for the end of the Top 40 before paying any attention to Bouaffesse's motions. When the latter drily ordered him to maneuver his truck under the tamarind tree, the albino protested that slavery had been abolished, that he was only here because he was a nice guy, besides, my boss that's not you . . . *Name and service number!* roared the Chief Sergeant getting his notebook out, and his voice diffused such vibration that the albino turned red and his incipient sweat—can't even joke around—unglued the glasses from his flat nose. The fire-and-rescuemen unfolded their stretcher again while the albino placed the swinging hook above Solibo. The Chief Inspector stood in full sunlight like a tourist. The albino, seeing Jambette and Diab-Anba-Feuilles put ropes around the body, became indignant: What?! that's what you called me out for?! . . . Embarrassed laughter: everyone looked away so that someone else might feel free to jump in and explain. *A winch for a body!* the albino persisted. *What's up, is this a joke?* . . . The Chief Sergeant came near him with an awful buddy-buddy smile and bet a hundred francs that he wouldn't be able to lift the body up an inch despite his big muscles, so that the albino, eager at the prospect, hurried toward it, took a minute to chase the ants away, knotted the ropes around one of his hands, and without any further ceremony transported to the stretcher a body lighter than sugar cane ashes. (Bouaffesse roared: Mothercrocker! . . . —as expected.)

Moreover, denying the evidence, the Chief Sergeant grabbed the ropes tied to the body, which now came so easily to him that the policeman almost fell back. He cautiously retracted one hand, then a thumb, then an index finger; soon he held Solibo on his little finger to the complete stupefaction of all. At last he began to twirl the body, which mesmerized everyone. By simply twisting his wrist, Bouaffesse now switched the body to his middle finger, then his thumb, from the thumb to the index, from the index to the middle, spellbound by Solibo effortlessly floating in his loose ties. Diab-Anba-Feuilles wanted to try this for himself, so did Jambette and the fire-and-rescuemen, and from pinky to pinky this amusement provoked such hysterical agitation (nervous laughter, twitching) that the towtruck guy left amid general indifference. The Chief Inspector was left out of this delirium, but he was really in no better shape: soaked in an unhealthy sweat, he looked like one of those poor old blackmen that you come upon at the police station every day making impossible statements about running into devils and zombies.

Despite the window grille, its dirty glass, and the darkness in which we take increasingly greater gulps of dwindling air, we see them poke fun at the Magnificent. Sidonise, Sucette, Ti-Cal, and a few others weep over him, the others brood over mute sorrows. It's clear that we are no longer on the right side of life. In dying, Solibo plunged us where words become worthless and things are senseless. There, the sun and the tamarind trees stand, the heat beats down, all around the immobile Savanna life has taken refuge in air-conditioned shadows. Everything's there, familiar, but life is zilch. *What's happening to us, Lord? What's happening? . . .* La Fièvre's question hovers eternally in the van, and we turn toward him, given that he's usually mute. He's a featureless man, at the intersection of some fourteen ethnicities whose traits he has carefully avoided. We know him without knowing him, he's from Fort-de-France but he's not from here, and even his Creole has creoles from elsewhere in it. Ma Gnam's burial might have turned out sad, he recalls. Her children had gone across the water, destination Paris, with the help of Bumidom.[1] News of them came only on cards without envelopes. On Sunday afternoon, when the heat forced open every shutter, Ma Gnam hauled her stool out to her doorstep, spread her postcards on the bottom of an upturned pan in front of her, and so traveled with her children in the snows of the great country. Solibo Magnificent often came to sit at her side and traveled too. He was the only one able to dissipate that serpentine languor that beset Ma Gnam. She didn't have much spirit left, she barely ate, and no longer cursed the cars that honked by her windows. No mother can bear her children leaving for far away, but in the old blackwomen, continually wrestling on the border of some abyss, it provoked immediate drowning, noiseless, without a call for help, like those triumphant roosters which die once retired from the fighting pit. Ma Gnam died silently, choked by bitterness. If Solibo Magnificent hadn't found her before the police, her burial could have been real sad. We would have seen her at the morgue chapel, chemically treated like a starfish dried for tourists, with the white garment of the hospital's destitute and the mechanical Latin of a passing priest. Solibo told the whole market and proposed that we meet for a wake. We're not going to let her go like that, he kept repeating. Already at that time, wakes no longer existed except in the memory of tradition fanatics. Solibo didn't grieve for tradition, but Ma

---

[1]French Overseas Migration Bureau.

Gnam was from the days of storytelling and wakes, and she had braided so many sorrows lately that none of those who loved her could have let her go over to the other side with just a doctor's death certificate, a plot number from the city hall, and a ride to the cemetery without even a procession through her country's streets. With the help of Ma Goul (an ancestral merchant) and Ma Elo (queen of the macadam* dish), Solibo Magnificent took care of everything. Ma Gnam was bathed in herb-scented water, dressed in her Sunday madras. Solibo hid the mirrors, swept the house, and ruined himself to cover the expenses: the coffin, the candles, the rum, the syrup, the lemons, the coffee, and one or two bags of soup vegetables. In the evening a group of women with memories came to rest their old bones around the body in Ma Gnam's room. With the fervor and the quivering of old age, they sang and recited their service songbooks until morning: *Once dead, once dead, sinner, you shall live again, and once dead, the Lord will judge you*—and now Solibo brought a pot of coffee—*in the old days, Lord, heedless, cursing the flame of your law, alas vainglory!*—and now Solibo offered bowls of clear broth—*Once the old days are gone all become humble again, Almighty God! If you would forgive us, our tears would dry.* And Solibo, ecstatic, brought out the tin cups and bowls of soup again. A group of men had piled up in the kitchen, so many that they spilled out into the street. One or two big fellows got the drums out and shattered the night with a stampede of heartbeats. And they parted the thick skin of their mouths to shout some: Hooo Solibooo, what's the deal, does the rum belong to the bottle?! . . . or: Hooo Ma Gnam, tell us who you gave the seven lumps, elephant legs, and ball pain to?! . . . And they laughed like trumpets. Every couple minutes, someone got up to put in their two cents about Ma Gnam: My children, she liked to suck on three things: her pipe every night, vermouth every Sunday, and rum all the time! ... Their thick laughs underscored their useless words ... Eyes streamed for joy. Rum and soup went down bottomless throats. But, of course, some respectable blackmen left their beds to fling insults from their windows, 'cause, shit! just because you bastards don't have to be noplace tomorrow morning you shouldn't stop everybody else from getting some sleep! Their insults produced no effect; they must have grabbed their hallo-hello! since the police was there in no time. The patrol chief, wild-eyed, demanded: And just what do you call the hullabaloo you're making here, huh? ... (Thank God, it wasn't Bouaffesse!) Solibo Magnificent then got on stage. *Oh language, master of all things!* The cops were speechless before him. Mouths and drums fell silent. His voice whirled, ample, then thin, broken, then warm, mellow, then crystal or shrill, and rounding off with low cavernous tones. A voice splitting with caresses, tears, enchantments, imperial and sobbing, and shaking with murmurs, dipping or fluttering along the frontiers of silent sound. Only some echo of the old women singing could be heard when, in order to breathe, he swallowed a couple of words. That's how he celebrated Ma Gnam, in grand style. Her life and her tribulations were told, recognized, wept over. Every recess of her good heart was brought to light. It was the second police van, led by a French officer, which broke the spell over the first cops, gave away two hundred billyclub blows, and scooped up a queue of bleeding blackmen, Solibo himself among them. In the central jail, in front of us, he cried nia nia nia about not being able to be there for Ma Gnam's burial—but never, not ever, did that jail that I know so well resound with so much laughter, songs, riddles, and jokes, and words, words, words ... Now all of this gathers in my head into one memory: Ma Gnam had a nice funeral. Without the Magnificent, she would have left like a dog, like him right now . . .

By falling silent, La Fièvre rousts us back to our ill-luck, where the policemen are still having their fun with Solibo. Like us, Congo watches, shuts the skin over his eyes, steps back, returns to the window to watch again. Suddenly, while La Fièvre has resumed his ghostly silence, Congo pushes us away violently. He breaks the window pane with his forehead. His bleeding face crashes against the grille. *Oala pan hespé,* so there's no respect any more?! . . . Filled to the brim with painful silence, we howl along with him.

The noise of the smashed window and Congo's screams broke the hypnosis. Thrown toward the stretcher, the body of the Magnificent landed there like a bubble. Pilon, standing still in the blazing sun, was interested solely in the body, the Chief Sergeant and his acolytes charged raging to the van with Zulu screams and opened its doors, billyclubs for banners, jumping with impatience. But Bouaffesse wanted to savor the moment: Let's not get excited here, pleeze . . . With the witnesses piled up in the back, Congo was standing alone near the broken window, fierce, the blood from his face flooding his shoulders. You again, Papa, creaked Bouaffesse, so you're the mad dog of the group? You don't even have good manners under all that white hair?! I make nice, I put you in the béké's car while I wait for the Inspector to take care of all the details of legal procedure and you, like an unbaptized savage, you break the window and you curse the urban population but nevertheless cause urban disorder?! *Get out here!* . . . The old man stood ramrod before the Chief Sergeant, braving him with his eyes, under the nightmare gaze of Jambette and Diab-Anba-Feuilles, and the witnesses still packed together. Why you do that, Papa? Bouaffesse asked.

—*Pani hespé, pani lavi, hi bray!*[1]

—Ho, Diab, what's he drooling here?

—He says that people can't live without respect, chief!

Bouaffesse walked up to him until he touched the belly of the old man's dry body: Respect, respect, you're the one talking respect? I, I am a man of respect who respects your white hair, otherwise I would have already broken your head on the masonry! No, oh no, where is my mother Stéphanise to see this?! An old blackman who comes from I don't know where and stands in front of me and talks respect! God, Lord! Me, I respect everything: Jesus Christ, the Pope, our Mother Republic, Social Security, Air France, the National Bank of Paris, and even the Martinican Cooperative Bank, I respect the Law, Philosophy, World Peace, NATO, de Gaulle, the Peugeot 604 and even the two-cylinder, I respect Schœlcher,* Félix Eboué, Joan of Arc, the coolies, I don't like Haitians but dammit I respect them! You, you're a stray dog, where's your respect?! You came out of your woods to poison a poor chap in the Savanna who never did you wrong and you come talk to me about respect?! Well, know that despite your white hair, I'm going to crush your eggs, because I know that you're the one who poisoned Solibo, I don't know with what, but I know it's you, and in the name of the Law, I'm going to crush your onions until you tell me what you killed him with! ... The old man suffered the assault without budging. Pilon intervened: Please, Bouaffesse, don't get in the way of procedure! The word *procedure* always dumped a bucket of cold water on the Chief Sergeant. Cooled off, he made a sign to his men to put away their clubs and then turned his antennae toward

---

[1] [No respect, no life, that's the truth!]

the fire-and-rescuemen who were having their turn spinning Solibo around above the stretcher. Their joy crashed against the police-report face of Chief Sergeant Bouaffesse, and they mumbled some vague appeasing things. The Chief Sergeant noted in an official voice that their intemperance with the principal body of a criminal inquiry could get them charged with misappropriation of a cadaver for purposes none too Roman nor Apostolic. With a studied slowness, he took down their civil status and then meanly ordered them to bring the body to Dr. Lélonette. The ambulance took off. The squealing of tires drowned out part of the declaration Inspector Pilon addressed to the witnesses. Congo had gone back inside the van and was pressing on his forehead. The departure of Bouaffesse and the other uniforms seemed to have thawed out the group, and all of us came near the doors that Pilon kept open. The grave and overwhelming inculpatory evidence gathered gives us probable cause to extend your custody, the Inspector was repeating, during which your hearings will be continued at the police station. This silenced and, yes, even stunned those now called suspects.

Chapter 4

My friends, enough!

Pilon sees that the preliminary investigation

was but criminal

(Weep?

For Congo.)

The suspects were   unloaded in the courtyard
                         of the police station in the
early afternoon. As usual during Carnival, everyone was
out patrolling the streets and the building was empty. Inspectors and superintendents, metropolitans for the most
part, dropped by the office in the morning, and then, chang-
ing into flower-print shirts and Bermuda shorts, left to hunt
down our carnivalesque mores for their scrapbooks. The
suspects had to empty their pockets (a small bottle of holy
water, a crucifix, bits of a rosary, a few coins, a Pepsi bottle-
cap, two hairpins, a pair of scissors, three magnets, a notebook, a pencil . . .) before the police chief who had relieved
Bouaffesse of his shift (named Albert Raffine, nicknamed
Cold Shivers), repeat their civil status, and wait in line until
Chief Sergeant Raffine (whose handwriting couldn't reach
zero miles per hour) had recorded everything into the
custody log. By the time they finally got to sit down on
the seal-stamped benches of the Department of Criminal
Investigation, the afternoon was stretching its tall shadows.
The deserted building was already adding an inexhaustible
echo to the clamor of the vidés . . .

From his desk, Evariste Pilon phoned the superintendent in vain, and tried, without any more success, to reach
one of the records clerks. The clerks had done their best to
free up their afternoon: a file lay in plain view on the desk.
Pilon opened it and quickly read:

Archivist's note to Chief Inspector E. Pilon:

- Name of the victim (with some reservations): Prosper *Bajole*. Born approximately 192? in Sainte-Marie.

- Dossier: three arrests for public intoxication, willful assault and battery on a police officer . . . several visits to the Central Prison.

- Nota: no official document confirms his civil status—something not unusual around here. *Solibo*: was that his only nickname? Such information would help me get further details.

The file consisted of some old criminal dossiers, two anthropometric shots in which the victim appeared younger, a topographical survey of the area around the tamarind tree on which the locations of the body and the objects taken for evidence were numbered, a list of these objects, enlarged fingerprints, blank forms, and pictures of the body. Everything was still nice and neat as was every file at the beginning of every investigation and yet soon to be smudged and shapeless, enclosing within it a fragment of the Chief Inspector's life. Pilon got someone to pour him some coffee, which he sipped without sugar while making a few phone calls: Hello, golden chabine? yeah, it's Vara, I'm not going to be able to make it to the vidés with you and the children, a murder, yes, my shift's over but I want to finish with this thing, just four or five hours, don't wait for me. —Hello? Dr. Lélonette, please . . . he's not in yet? . . . yes, yes, I sent it to you, murder, he was killed last night in the Savanna, not in Guadeloupe, yes, I know, the ants on him are usually found in Guadeloupe, but I swear to you that he's from the Savanna, right in the middle of Fort-de-France, tell Dr. Lélonette to begin the autopsy as soon as possible, I suspect it's poisoning . . . tell him to hurry, I'll take care of getting permission from the district attorney's office. Hello? Dr. Viantot? oh, he's not there . . . did you get my samples? good . . . only the alcohol content . . . the usual report . . . He had barely put down the phone when his doorbell rang, it was Chief Sergeant Bouaffesse, wishing to integrate a few direct quotes in Creole into the report on the Doudou-Ménar incident, since you told me yourself that it was a language, right? . . .

—Look, who gives a damn, Sergeant: Justice hasn't gotten there yet . . .

Finally, Pilon got to his paperwork. He filled out and signed the custody logbook. He wrote out his report on the visit to the scene of the crime, and then another about the whole affair, which he went to drop off on the superintendent's desk. He completed a few forms, wrote out notes summarizing the four files which lay on his desk, and stacked them on top of his file cabinet. Finally, on a long sheet of graph paper, he wrote down the name of every suspect and opposite, in parentheses, he put illegible remarks, dots, stars, and small x's . . . Ladies and gentlemen, in front of this list Pilon's brain heated up like a Fiat 600. Each name brought back details of the Q&A, innocuous gestures, certain looks, imperceptible attitudes. You'd really think the smart policeman had a Kodak in his head that recorded a little movie, not pornographic but personal, whose sounds, colors, frames, and angles definitely operated within the strictures of the art of policing when it comes to criminal matters. He drew diagrams with arrows going up and down, circled names, underlined others, called up the archivist, and completed his sinister geometrical map. Sometimes he snatched up photos of the body, gloomily examined them while smoothing his hair under his bakoua.

Confusion filled his eyes when he took out his lens to scrutinize the ants, or even when, hands on his temples, he recalled the episode of the body gaining weight or becoming lighter than the brain of a drunk hairdresser full of absinthe at five in the morning. The phone rang often: Chief Sergeant Raffine who worried about getting the right signature on the custody papers, the superintendent himself who, from an imperial terrace, inquired about the "death in the Savanna" and promised to get authorization from the on-duty deputy public prosecutor to perform the autopsy, and finally Bouaffesse, noting the zeal of Diab-Anba-Feuilles and Jambette, who were eager to be of service despite the end of their shifts. Evariste Pilon accepted, rolled up his sleeves, and soon opened his office door for the Chief Sergeant. Head bare, shirt open, Bouaffesse carried a plastic bag with victuals. In the hall, Jambette and Diab-Anba-Feuilles, with an air of importance, placed a bench for four of the suspects. Bouaffesse was cheerful, keener than a hunter under a flight of teals: he was going to make sure that this investigation got somewhere, hell yeah!

Who killed Solibo? The writer with the curious bird name was the first suspect to be interrogated. He spoke for a long, long time, with the sweat and the pace of blackmen in a pickle. No, not writer: *word scratcher,* it makes a huge difference, Inspekder, the writer is from another world, he ruminates, elaborates, or canvasses, the word scratcher refuses the agony of oraliture, he collects and transmits. It's almost symbolic that I was there to hear the Magnificent's last word. He hadn't told me about the performance, I just waited for him every night, and on the third he was there . . . I knew him without knowing him, he had agreed to meet a few times with me in the market or in the bars. I dedicated my book to him, but he never really got interested in me . . . He wasn't interested either in my plans to write about his life: writing for him caught nothing of the essence of things. I don't see it that way. Here, we stand in friction between worlds, Inspekder, in an eroding space, a crumbling space where . . .

—Enough philosophy! Bouaffesse cut in, tell us instead if Solibo ate something under the tamarind tree . . .

But the writer added nothing new. Solibo Magnificent hadn't swallowed anything, no one had come near him, he had fallen by himself, et cetera. No he didn't have any enemies, no he didn't have an exact address, no he barely knew any of the other suspects. He stood by his statement, reread it, backed it up, and signed. Bouaffesse left his typewriter to push him out into the hall: Come on, forward march, good-for-nothing! Next . . .

Who killed Solibo? The "Syrian," a Lebanese bastard child named Zozor Alcide-Victor, seemed more at ease and insisted on speaking of Solibo in general terms in order to enlighten the conversation because he was a great man, Mr. Inspector. His life was the nourishment for dozens of others. He wasn't the kind of man who meddles in other people's business, but if you ever told him you were sick at heart, even a little, he always stood by you. His spiritual balance set him apart. I've been practicing the martial arts for eons. Without being what one could call a master in that domain, I have nonetheless reached a certain level in it. My meeting with Mr. Solibo occurred under peculiar circumstances. One night, in the Savanna, where I was taking some fresh air, right under the Desnambuc statue. Three drunks approached. Two of them pushed me, insulting me. The third was pissing, standing a little further away under a tamarind tree. I wasn't above using my fighting skills. Today it would be different. The martial arts quickly cease to be a weapon and become an awakening of the spirit, a nonbeing which integrates the universe, a peace. So I take care of the first two drunks and go toward the third. He had shown no aggressiveness, but I wanted to neutralize him too. The art of war demands that all potential enemies be preempted. So, I come nearer. The third drunk was this Mr. Solibo. A few steps away from him, I realized that he was not drunk. Not one bit. He was all dressed up, with a ridiculous little hat from some grade B detective flick. I came closer. Only then did I make him out. Head high, he was smiling, but in his eyes there was deep concentration. Before me I saw controlled breathing, a spirit in a state of silence, a relaxed body flowing with free energy. I lost all desire to fight, I was immobile, vanquished, as if standing on the edge of a cliff. Thinking he was a martial arts adept, I greeted him as such and acknowledged my defeat according to the rules. Breaking into laughter, with his extraordinary voice, Inspector, he said to me: What are you talking about, come drink a little something with Solibo . . . Voilà. Ever since, I have always lent an attentive ear to his fits of words, his ever-refreshing glossolalia, but I don't know any more than that about him. A drink of punch when fate made us meet, a few jobs done for my store . . . The Syrian expressed himself in a composed voice, which leaned on the r's and ran after the Creole i's. With mannered gestures, he underlined the important words with his thin hand and checked constantly on the folds of his shirt. No enemy, no address, Solibo hadn't swallowed a thing and no one had come near him. He hadn't been standing under the tamarind just waiting for Solibo, since it was also his meeting place with an adorable girl who, incidentally, didn't show up . . . A whole lot of trouble over a heart attack, he concluded, signing his statement.

—Why do you suspect it was cardiac arrest?

—How else would you explain such a sudden death?

—By some Arab poison your dad would've taught you! Bouaffesse proposed.

The Syrian left with a little less pep in his step.

Who killed Solibo? During the Q&A's, the Chief Inspector stood by the window, chewing a french fry, or gulping down juice. He asked the questions in a friendly voice and reformulated the answers in neat and concise sentences that Bouaffesse transcribed into the report. The suspects were desperately hanging on every one of Pilon's tranquil poses. They turned their heads in his direction, trying to drown their eyes in his, for the bluish mass of the Chief Sergeant sitting across from them emanated a constant threat, brewing under the uniform. Pilon picked up on this while interrogating the next suspect: Justin Hamanah, nicknamed Didon, jobber at the vegetable market. Knotted with muscles, the coolie walked in stiffly, sat on the edge of the chair and, eyes lost on a Bouaffesse attentive to his typewriter keys, he whispered his answers to the questions. What are you saying now? asked an anxious Bouaffesse. A-argh! an agonized trumpet sound came forth. The smell of red beans fermented with some old rum in a mixture of decomposed goat meat and boiled yams infested the air of the room. The coolie hadn't moved, but he shivered, gnashed his teeth, and stared at Bouaffesse with eyes like a broken anthill. The Chief Inspector and the Chief Sergeant both leapt for the window only to be met by the stifling air outside, already stuffy from the heat of Carême. Bouaffesse was the first to recover and came back to the suspect: You killed him, didn't you, that's why you're shitting all over yourself, ANSWER! . . . Water swelled the coolie's eyes and ran down his cheeks: *An pa tchoué pêson,* I killed no one . . . Pilon watched calmly. In his diagrams, the name of the coolie had been neither circled nor underlined, and his files mentioned only something about the theft of a hen near Tivoli. During his first hearing, in the Savanna, he had declared that he knew Solibo Magnificent well (I carted his charcoal for him), with such respect that the Chief Inspector hadn't pressed further. Nostrils gripped by the Sergeant's evil hand (What kind of poison did you give him, coolie poison?), twisting on his sodden chair, mute despite Bouaffesse's roaring, the coolie had simply reached the rock bottom of all terror. Pilon opened the door and beckoned to Diab-Anba-Feuilles, who dragged him down the hall. With two fingers, Bouaffesse pushed the soiled chair away. Here you go, son, he said to Jambette, Merry Christmas.

—You're frightening them . . .
—Me?
—Yeah.
—You're talking like I was Dracula with his two big teeth . . .
—I need them to talk, to talk a lot, not get petrified . . .
—Fine. I'll wear my Palm Sunday face . . .

When the coolie came back, almost cleaned up, Bouaffesse's unexpected smile had the same effects: trumpets, stench, shivers, et cetera. Without a word, Diab-Anba-Feuilles led him off by the collar again. Next! sighed Pilon.

—It's the no-good prostitute, announced Bouaffesse.

Who killed Solibo? The woman named Conchita Juanez y Rodriguez, claiming to be Colombian, knew no more than the others. Her thick hair was sculpted around her shoulders in perfumed, blue-black waves. Her ruined make-up caked around her eyes, her lips and cheeks no longer concealed her fatigue or her age, but her natural grace was still moving. She knew Solibo like she did the night-walkers of Fort-de-France, blackmen with no address, who flirted with night life in the torch-lit venues of the serbi game, on the park benches, at the brothels, and who were more elusive than rivers in the thirsty South. The shadows transformed their monotonous life, and the moon's pregnant light revealed that there were as many paths in the town as there were in the forest with all its freedom. At night the Colombian saw Solibo and several others regularly . . . He liked your stuff, Bouaffesse sneered . . .

—Nooo, he came to see the Saraïbean . . .

—The Caribbean? . . .

Solibo haunted brothels, never saying no to a night when he could afford it. Most often he went from prostitute to prostitute, each one showing him her special ways: Ah, here comes Margaret from St. Lucia, and here's Haiti, tell us about Haiti, Roselita, Mama! This is Clara from Dominica, and here's Puerto Rico *como esta uste?* Well I'll be damned! Who's this, is it Sacha from Barbados . . . the whole Caribbean's here! the Caribbean is here! . . . Without having been in these countries, breaking the bones of isolation in his mind, Solibo Magnificent could talk about them and talk and talk . . . These women's secrets, their ways of tasting the night were enough for the storyteller to describe each land, each people, each pain. Even the women from Brazil, from Chile, from Colombia like Conchita were astonished by his knowledge of the Other America.

—So he read a color-illustrated Larousse dictionary! Bouaffesse let loose, shrugging his shoulders.

—Nooo, 'e use to say: Meeserry draws ze saym way everry weyer . . .

—She said that all the time Solibo used to say: Misery draws the same way everywhere.

You're letting her get away with too many useless words, you know that?! said Bouaffesse, getting mad. He seized Conchita's chin, forced her eyes into his, and asked her if Solibo had swallowed anything under the tamarind. The prostitute said yes—and Bouaffesse, who was about to type in the answer, was stunned. The Chief Inspector came closer. 'E drraank frroom ze beeg rrom bohttle wiz ze ozers, confirmed Conchita and added: 'E olso eeet som candy grepfroots ... Solibo had rinsed his throat with the demi-john's rum once in a while and in the middle of the night had yelled: Doudou-Ménar, Let me taste your candied grapefruit so that some sugar will go down past my sweet tooth! ... The Fat One had brought him the sweet.

—YO PRI, WE GOT 'EM! roared Bouaffesse, they poisoned him with the grapefruit!

The Chief Sergeant and the Chief Inspector congratulated each other while Conchita Juanez y Rodriguez watched them, glowing beatific that she could have helped them.

Bouaffesse rolls downstairs like an agricultural day worker to the hiring yard. He crosses the hall where the first victims of the dirty vidés (tourists clobbered by the offended objects they were trying to take a picture of, blackmen in suit plus tie minus checkbook ...) are glued to the counter, then rushes into the courtyard, toward a garbage can. Bouaffesse almost jumps into it, goes through scraps of crumpled paper, wine and rum bottles, dried ink pads, trace paper, old typewriter ribbons, stale fried dough, dried tears, dust balls crystallizing the leftover pain spilling from police records. Suddenly, he finds a translucent, yellowish crumb, still powdered with some sugar: the remains of the candied grapefruit, the sole vestige of Doudou-Ménar's basket, pulverized during the battle against the night-shift policemen. (Children, no formality here between us: let's reread the part where Doudou-Ménar enters the police station to tell of Solibo's death—as homage, since at this hour she freezes in the morgue fridge.) Bouaffesse screams again: YO PRI!

The Chief Inspector, Evariste Pilon, had the piece of grapefruit brought immediately to the lab. Then he called the coolie back in. Despite the shower and the clean clothes given to him by Diab-Anba-Feuilles, some unbearable effluvium still wrapped itself around the unfortunate man. Bouaffesse typed his statement with one hand and held his nose with the other, while Pilon questioned him with his head out the window. The coolie hadn't seen Solibo eat the candied grapefruit, nor even drink from the demijohn. If there had been a five-centime coin on the floor, you'd've seen it though, no? Bouaffesse said through his nose.

—Heh heh heh heh, the coolie chortled painfully, on the verge of a nervous breakdown.

Pilon made him tell him about his day, hour by hour, from his morning take-off punch to the gathering under the tamarind. If Solibo is dead on today's day, he whispered after a profound inspiration, it's by fate's hand, Inspekder, because no one had in his heart for him the kinds of burning that fed hatred. Solibo's words smoothed all bitterness and inspired respect . . . Then, as if the mere evocation of Solibo had given him courage, as if he could no longer resist a powerful urge, the coolie spoke of the charcoal: Inspekder, Solibo Magnificent sold charcoal at the vegetable market. He made his own charcoal, deep in the woods near Tivoli, with the permission of Ma Cyanise, the mulatto and common-law wife of two or three békés. These men had preferred to give her some plots of land here and there rather than legitimize any one of her many children. Ma Cyanise, who couldn't stand to see a blackman before her (she even pretended that her mother, who was as dark as the bottom of a pan, was a Carib Indian) . . . What was I saying? Oh yes, so Ma Cyanise, who got a rash when a blackman came near her, would never have allowed Solibo to dig charcoal ovens on her land. She wasn't a bad woman, but blackmen weren't for her nor for any of her girls. When once in a while one of them opened his mouth to ask: Ma Cyanise, pleeze, could I . . . ? she answered: *Sôti douvan mwen akré neg noué,* Out of my sight, you Negro blackman! . . . Heh heh heh, with her warm-vinegar voice, shivering because of old age, and her yellow mulatto skin that age crumples so easily, we all knew that deep down she was nice. She liked the békés, she liked the békés too much, but you see now, I wonder if seeking the blackman's life of mud would have really been the sign of a spirit made of lead. Had blackmen owned big white houses, with balcony and veranda, meat in the canari* every day, well I do think that Ma Cyanise would have also liked blackmen . . . So, it's Ma Florise, Solibo's mother, who got Ma Cyanise to agree to let her son build charcoal ovens. How? I don't know. Ma Florise was herself as black as yesterday's moonless night. (I only saw her once, near the Rochambeau barracks where she sold milk to the soldiers while Solibo, still a child then, washed the horses of the ranking officers) . . . What was I saying again? Forgive me, Inspekder, but here, in this place of Law, it's hard to keep a cool head. So Florise was black, but Ma Cyanise had nevertheless given her permission for the ovens. So you see now that deep down she was nice. After Ma Cyanise's death (not one of her békés had come to say one good thing about her during the wake, no, and not one came to sweat carrying her coffin! but how many blackmen were there, hm? all the blackmen came! all sorts who came to drink her rum! heh

heh heh. At the wake the storytellers kept asking the body: So Ma Cyanise, aren't you going to tell all these Negro blackmen to get out of your sight? Should we stay or should we go? ... Hee hee hee) ... What was I saying? Oh yes, after her death, her heirs didn't bother with the ovens. Solibo began to sell charcoal at the market. You wouldn't have run into him, Inspekder, since you probably use gas for cooking. But folks who cooked otherwise knew him. He measured the charcoal he sold with an empty margarine pot, two centimes a pot when it was centimes, one franc when it was francs. He used to wear black flour-sacking. His panama hat, older than misfortune, fell on his ears. He really looked like a coolie without a contract. But when he was done with his charcoal business, putting away the leftovers under a stall, he put on his polyester pants. Now he was a man with class, not a blackman dressed up for mass, but a blackman with class. In those hours, the women vendors basked around him like lizards in the sun. He wasn't one of those pretty-blackmen-with-no-balls, genuine style coiled inside him. Even under his sacking, his old panama hat, and his dirty linen, he stood with strength, and you could hardly walk away after buying your charcoal so much did his words glue you to his stall zwlip zwlip ... I don't want to think about him being dead, Inspekder ... Well, I just wanted to tell you about Solibo and his charcoal: it was no breadfruit-wood or camasey charcoal that smothers your fire with ash, no. It was a resounding crystal, spitting fire like a blowtorch: a charcoal made of logwood, wild sage, and mixed with ox-eye wood. It was no accident that he sold charcoal, since that's what he was in our lives: the charcoal is the wood, it's the trunk, the branches and leaves, and also the root—and the charcoal is no longer the wood because it's the flame and the fire, imagine the magic of fire and sap,

of the bark, of the ash, of the root and the dust ... Between
the forest and the flames, Inspekder, that's where charcoal
stands, and you know what Solibo used to say in that bitter
voice in which he spoke during his last days? Child, right in
between the forest and the flames stands Solibo ... So what
enemy, what poison are you talking about? ...

But the Inspector was barely listening to him, and
Bouaffesse was recentering his typewriter.

Evariste Pilon called back the writer, the prostitute,
and the Syrian, questioned them about their day, and tried
in vain to make them recall Solibo drinking or eating. He
wrote down the places where they said they had had a
drink, the streets where they had wandered, the benches on
which they had slept. He asked them to name someone re-
lated to Mr. Solibo in any way, friend, brother, anyone who
could possibly get him his address or the name of a possible
enemy, could say more about him ... The Chief Inspector
carefully wrote down the names they gave him. When he
decided to send them back to the holding pen, the coolie's
legs were shaking. Without trying to understand anything,
Diab-Anba-Feuilles grabbed him by the hair and dragged
him down the hall. The other suspects didn't protest at all.
(Was it because Bouaffesse, who hadn't said a word yet,
looked like he was out for blood?)

Drriiingg!
—Pilon, here ... Ah, Dr. Lélonette, how are you? ...
Yes ... I don't want to spoil your Carnival but I've got thirteen suspects in custody ... I need the autopsy results as
soon as possible ... I want the perpetrators by tomorrow
night ... yes ... no ... poison, presumably ... Not likely?
Well, I do have some concrete indications ... Look, we're

going to help you out here: in his stomach, you're going to find a piece of candied fruit . . . it's all there . . . tomorrow, around noon? I'll be there . . . yes . . . yes some manioc ants . . . yes, I know . . . curious, but there's worse . . .

Till the first blushes of the sky, the Chief Inspector and the Chief Sergeant question the seven other suspects:

1

Pierre Philomène Soleil, nicknamed Pipi, told of his day with astonishing precision: the level of his first glass of rum, the number of jobs he did in the morning, and the squares of breadfruit swallowed around noon. He talked about the real bad vidé in which he took part, mentioned the streets he cruised, song after song until the one where he collapsed under the tamarind with a demijohn of tafia. Then Solibo's cry, his fall, and everybody waiting around for Doudou-Ménar's return: Yes we could have waited for her until the middle of Carême, like in the song, but what a wait, Inspekder, and what pain! Nothing was the same for us, Solibo's body was stuck, undoing our life, calling out to it, weighing it, and you know how much life here is worth when we place it in front of death. So as a way to escape we stood over the body to cull a few memories and share them like the fruits of the season: we were using memory as oxygen, to live, to survive . . .

In front of the somewhat disconcerted policemen, Pipi answered the questions in uninterrupted sentences, their echoes demonstrably resounding in him. Nooo, Solibo didn't have enemies, no more than the yams or the sun do, no he didn't know Solibo's exact address because the only thing that mattered was to know if a man had a heart and where it stood in his chest . . . Then bending toward Pilon, he said: I don't want to tell you how to run your investigation (you're a masterpiece of policework, and I know that), but to look for who killed Solibo can get at no truth. The real question is: Who is Solibo? . . . When you add: And why Magnificent? . . . , then you're talking. Because that's where we must plow up the real questions. We must question this earth, this sea, this sky, the curve of this hill, the name of that street, the horizon on which unknown countries sometimes cast their shadows. Have you ever examined the shape of your nose, your too-long legs? your own name? What have you asked of that name yet: Pilon? Do you know whether it brings you back the memory of an ancestor, a maroon blackman they would have hobbled? And whether the booboo got infected and they had to amputate his leg? And whether the plantation slaves nicknamed him Lil' Pestle, Ti-Pilon! Ti-Pilon! because of some wood he attached to his stump? It makes your heart jump, no? Well, I found this out from Solibo: to learn to question, no more certainties or evidence, but the question, the whole question. That's what Solibo was about. You understand the "Magnificent" part?

The Chief Inspector and the Chief Sergeant let him speak, almost despite themselves, more interested in the jobber's curious personality than in what he was saying. They had in front of them a real man who looked them in the eye and who didn't inspire the desire to grab or yell at him. Pipi had no memory of anyone approaching Solibo under the tamarind or even if the latter had swallowed anything or not, because the essential thing to see or hear was Papa's words: the things he *said*. (This was followed by a mighty elaboration of the Magnificent's words; that part got on Bouaffesse's nerves.) Among the suspects, he knew only

Didon the coolie and Charlo' the musician; he once met the Oiseau who wrote all the time. He wasn't as close to Solibo as Sucette the drum man was, but he insisted on speaking only about what the Master was like in the good old days. After a short silence, Pilon asked him for a few names, people who would be able to give more information about the victim, then handed him his statement which he signed with two X's, bitter tears in his eyes.

2

The one called Bête-Longue spent more time getting the questions explained to him than answering them. His day and what he could possibly have seen during the fatal night remained mysteries despite Bouaffesse's threats and shouting. About the Magnificent he became more eloquent, his eyes even shining, as if he'd just surfaced after drowning of boredom. He wasn't Solibo's enemy, Solibo and he were good friends, on the contrary, no he hadn't run into Solibo in his last hours because Solibo hadn't sold charcoal that day. During Carnival, the market slows down, Inspekder, the merchants come down late and go back up early. The customers save their pennies to buy candies later at the Carnival. On that day the Magnificent usually returns to his ovens near Tivoli, on the lands of the late Cyanise. That's probably what he did on that fatal day, Inspekder. I'd be surprised if he saw anyone. Beside his oven, Solibo would become a tree. He could stand et cetera hours without moving, speaking to himself in his head. I'm telling you this because that's how I saw him in the last few days, with my own eyes. Looking for my rattraps, I lost my way in these woods, somewhere around his ovens, and I saw him through some bushes. Sitting in the smoke. Stiff. His lips moving silently. He must have been telling himself some terrible things about life here. His joy, his swagger seemed gone. I was looking at a man in pain, like the ones your police pick up out of those gutters in Terres-Sainville. It was really painful to see that. What's the use, Lord, of showing some things? I tiptoed away to go home and milk my rum bottle. I was so out of it that Jeanne-Yvette, my girlfriend, thought I had stumbled on a forest she-devil. I sat mute, before and after her questions. Inspekder, there are some sailors who let an early nightfall trap them at sea, no moon, no stars. And yet, gripping that misfortune by the collar, they continue to sail; they know that in the direction of men, a fire among the hutches on the beach will show them the way . . . They latch their lives to that fire and draw courage from it. For us, Solibo Magnificent was exactly that. A light on the horizon which breathes *Tjenbé rèd! Tjenbé rèd!*[1] and which helps you make it just by being there. So how could I admit to Jeanne-Yvette that I had seen him as distressed as one of us, in the net of misfortune? I dragged around my sorrow for days until I ran into him under the tamarind. I was so happy to see him apparently doing OK. Laughing with strength, blowing words into the wind. So how can you think I could have killed him? Or even that someone from here could have done such a thing? I don't want to show you how to do your job, forgive me Inspekder, but I've been dragging about in Fort-de-France's mud for about forty years now, I know what all the gangsters, what all those godless boys, those blackmen who respect nothing, are capable of . . . So you want to know my feeling about this? It costs me nothing to tell you: in this country, Inspekder, no one kills storytellers (*yo paka senyien majolè isiya*) . . .

---

[1] [Hold on tight!]

3

Sosthène Versailles, nicknamed Ti-Cal, began with a solemn declaration: he was an anticolonialist militant from the Martinican Progressive Party, his detention was but a subterfuge to sabotage the next municipal election campaign, at this time he should be meeting with his comrades from the grassroots[1] to discuss the fundamental distinction Césaire established between *in-dependence* and *un-dependence*. Concerning Solibo, who could have possibly wanted to kill him? He was a good man who knew how to enjoy life. I even sometimes scolded him for that. We're about to be extinct and I resist. Solibo too was resisting in his own way. Maybe with even more effect than my posters and pamphlets. I was always aware of his great consciousness, of his uneasiness. His tales never sought to transform anyone, as if he told them entirely for himself. He didn't judge. Neither those who repeat *Vive de Gaulle!* all day, nor the others like myself who bellow: Independence, Independence . . . Seeing him sip his noonday rum with such-and-such a Gallic blackman, seeming on friendlier terms with him than with me, I protested: How can you drink like that with so-and-so? . . . He would tell me laughing, Hey, calm down, son, the door sees on both sides of the house, and on each side of the door it's still the house . . . Without understanding everything he said, I felt that his assessments were broader than mine. I still reproached him for his taste for rum, for polyester, for over-ironed shirts. He liked shoes that shone like mirrors, his jaw dropped before cars, he never missed any zouk* or soccer game. And his taste in food? He loved the fritters, the marinades, the whole barbecued sheep which he scorched with tafia, féroces* at all hours, quite a

---

[1]The Martinican Progressive Party's basic structure.

performance, in which I must say he did give a piece of his conscious blackman's mind. In fact, he was more inscribed in the life here than any of us, he wasn't running after some mirage, he didn't turn away from himself, but profoundly explored what we are with tourist eyes, child's eyes. For those who couldn't see, he seemed a vain inscription in our little lives, alienated by Africa or France, so much so that at the time I said to him: Papa (we all instinctively called him Papa), you live like a man without foundation . . . He answered. Too much virtue is boring, son, and it does you no good, you know, to forget here in the name of Here, or life in the name of Life . . . So he was present everywhere, known and appreciated, no longer as a storyteller (for in his last seasons he spoke less and less—I don't know why, maybe age . . .) but as a nice guy . . .

Apart from that, Ti-Cal knew nothing. (*Vive de Gaulle!* Bouaffesse hollered as he signed his statement . . .)

4

Charles Gros-Liberté, nicknamed Charlo', answered the questions like a sleepwalker, stroking the white rash growing on his cheek. To help him relax, Pilon asked him what he knew about what the Magnificent did in the hours before his death—evoking Solibo seemed to loosen everyone's tongue. Charlo' said none of them could know such a thing: Solibo lived without clock and calendar and, above all, had no habits. He scheduled his life only around his charcoal, his noontime punch at Chez Chinotte, and All Saints Day when he honored his deceased mother Florise (shed a tear for her, dear God!) with Saint Anthony candles. Apart from that, it was a waste of time to wait for him where you expected to see him. He would have played his beguine out of time if he had been a musician, and his mazurka would never have been spiced in the same place. Yes, every day he sold his charcoal, but always in a different way: today he seriously wanted to babble behind his sacks, the next day he sat at a respectable distance and sold from afar, the day after that he began selling from the middle of his spread-out sacks. Other times, he realized what he did and said: It's to taste life better that I give it a new flavor every time! . . . What is there to understand, Inspekder? Regarding his drinks, at Chez Chinotte, he arrived regularly at noon, on the dot, but he would enter through the front door, the window, or the back. Sometimes you found his glass without having seen him coming or going. And more important: while every rummy settles on one weapon of choice, Solibo zigzagged through them like a butterfly. This time it was white rum, another day he hollered for dark rum or straw rum. In this glass, he wanted a finger of blond sugar, in that one a dash of brown sugar, a teardrop of syrup, or a string of honey, or else he ordered an always unexpected dry punch. The length of time he spent at Chez Chinotte was never the same, he'd stay there the length of a sip or for two hours. At dawn on All Saints Day, there was one certainty: atop Florise's grave he would light twelve Saint Anthonys that no draft could blow out. He was in the cemetery without being there. You could look for him for ten thousand years, go up and down Trabaut without even running into him, or stumble over him at every step, at every grave, in the shadow of every cross, more present at the feast of the dead than the twenty thousand candles. Besides those three times, again without any real season, it was no use trying to find out where Solibo was, Inspekder, or what he was doing . . .

Then Charlo' confirmed that the Magnificent had gotten a piece of grapefruit from Doudou-Ménar's hands. The rest made Pilon yawn . . .

5

Edouard Zaboca, nicknamed La Fièvre, didn't say jack that was comprehensible about his day (I went around offering my chains to the streets since I myself am more like a path on the horizon of the sea and of life . . .) nor about Solibo (Try to imagine him standing like a beautiful filao tree, Inspekder, when he was most alive . . .).

—Did you run into him during the day?

—You can run into the wind which comes from the horizon, but never into the horizon. And to think that we only get to meet our own life in the afterlife, but the question, Inspekder, is: What is life here? and what does one say faced with death?

—I'd like to shove this typewriter down his throat! roared Bouaffesse.

—Calm down, Chief Sergeant. Mr. Zaboca, try to make yourself clearer. Who do you know among the people currently in custody with you?

—I know Ma'am Sidonise, that is, the taste of her coconut sherbet through which you live anew . . . The truth is we don't know ourselves . . .

—I could arrange for you and my billyclub to get to know each other, Bouaffesse proposed, getting to his feet.

Pilon, poring over his diagrams, stopped him: It's no use, Chief Sergeant, right now he's not important . . . La Fièvre signed his statement with a very elaborate bit of graffiti.

6

Antoinette Maria-Jésus Sidonise seemed to carry thirteen bushels of misery on her small shoulders, all the burdens of age. She remained prostrate on her chair, deaf to Bouaffesse's shouting, so much so that Pilon had to sit near her, to the point of brushing against her, and speak softly to her. Little by little, she opened up, murmured some mhmm, some yes, some no, said she didn't know where Solibo lived, understood nothing of the question about any possible enemy, and almost passed out when asked if she had ever resented the storyteller for anything he had done to her. On the other hand, she was the only one to admit she knew all the suspects (They buy my sherbets . . .) and that she had seen Solibo during the day. Despite the Chief Inspector and Chief Sergeant's excitement, of that day she told only a confusing story about some sharkstew (on his diagrams, Pilon added an asterisk to her name: she had had lunch with the victim). When they tried to find out what followed the meal, Sidonise gave a start: How rude! What Solibo and I did is really none of your business. He left around two, I think he left to go check on his ovens. No, he didn't tell me he would be speaking under the tamarind. Chance, divine destiny, made me walk by there. Sucette fist-fought his drum, other people were waiting, I waited with them. Poison? What poison? In the sharkstew! . . . My God, Lord! . . . Their hypothesis sent her back into a fainting fit from which she didn't emerge. Upon leaving, Pilon said to Bouaffesse: Have her set aside, she's the element that connects all of the others . . . Thus, Sidonise didn't rejoin the others in the holding pen, plunging the other suspects into suffocating anxieties: They must have killed her! . . . The minute sherbet vendor was simply kept apart from them in an office, but they didn't find out about it until the next evening.

7

A dry chabin, all worked up, Richard Cœurillon cried before and after every question. He said he was weeping over Solibo, over life and death, that he had spent his day crying in a bar in the Sainte-Thérèse area, yes he knew Solibo, the great Solibo, a true blackman, no he hadn't met him that day, among the suspects, he only knew Madame Sidonise, what enemy? what enemy? ... No one could have killed him, Inspekder! And Solibo didn't have an enemy because no one could hold anything against him for long ... It's really simple: suppose a blackman, because of some story of jealousy, girlfriends, or serbi (three domains in which Solibo sometimes hurt a man's feelings), decides to go stick a knife into him. Suppose that this blackman hides himself behind the door of Chez Chinotte at Happy Hour to trap the Magnificent, or maybe he lurks for him at the market, crouched behind one of the charcoal bags, red eyes, uglier than an old woman's tub. Well, on that day, Inspekder, even if he went by there every day, *Solibo Magnificent doesn't show!* I've seen not one blackman killed that way but ten, twenty, thirty assaulted by someone jumping from a bush who plants his knife into his victim and runs away. But for Solibo it never worked: he didn't show! If he goes by your house every day to drink punch, and one day you put rat poison in his glass, that day Solibo doesn't show! What does it mean? Simply that despite his fat, generous laugh, his drinking, his verbal hurricanes, Solibo Magnificent lived life as we live war: always on his guard. Get the old békés to tell you stories about the maroon blackmen that no dog could track down. Men hiding in forests small as a hummingbird's nest but whom no creature could locate. The old hunters and the békés of bygone days called them *warriors!* Solibo Magnificent was of such a category. You can't kill these people, Inspekder. But I'm not done with your question: Solibo's enemies? They were defeated without battle, so they never brought it up again! Understand: imagine this man-killer waiting for the Magnificent with a knife. He waits here, Solibo goes there, he waits in front, Solibo comes through the back. Even better: he knocks the door down, but Solibo is no longer there! You see how he's in a pickle? The would-be killer would bemoan his own lot, watching where he put his feet, living the madness of rats inside demijohns: he would realize that though he couldn't find Solibo, the latter, on the other hand, would find him. In the middle of noon market the man would fall on his knees: Forgive me Solibo, forgive me Solibo! . . . Inspekder, I don't want it to look like I'm telling you some devilries, but at that exact moment, Solibo would appear as happy as a Guadeloupean at one of their cooks' festivals. He would comb the man-killer with his hand and say: Come have a drink with Solibo, my good man . . . The rest of the day you'd watch their drunken happiness grow around a rum bottle, better friends than if their blood had fed the same heart . . . Yes, he drank from the demijohn and ate some of the grapefruit. Can I go, Inspekder? I have twelve children waiting for me at home . . .

The first blushes of the sky. Night approaches and blows on the embers of the vidés: the last choruses rise. Despite the joyous riot that swarms within her, Fort-de-France squats in the shadows. Pilon and Bouaffesse smoke silently at a window. The Chief Sergeant checks out the Inspector from the corner of his eye. You'd swear that that Pilon carries a factory under his forehead. The thread which will lead to the guilty party now seems identified, but Bouaffesse has lost his footing: too many testimonies, too many stories, the puzzle's edges don't fit together in his head. He says: We should pull the canari out of the fire and taste the sauce in case there's too much salt . . .

—Should we figure out where we're at?

—Or where we're not, if you wish . . .

So, prodded by the Chief Sergeant's questions which induce early blooming in his thought process, the Chief Inspector unveils a long series of logic and deductions, fateful indeed, out of which no one escapes unscathed: Things are clearer, only some of the suspects (and not all of them as I first thought) held a grudge against the one named Solibo Magnificent, a man who seemed to arouse extreme feelings: admiration, which was often the case, or carefully concealed hatred. His enemies decide to poison him and go to the old quimboiseur named Congo. Just to make sure, they request two doses of poison (I get it! Bouaffesse exults), one for the sharkstew which Sidonise was supposed to get him to eat and the other for the candied grapefruit Doudou-Ménar was supposed to offer him under the tamarind. They set the trap with Sucette, the drum man, who also most certainly resented Solibo. Such a deployment is justified by Solibo Magnificent's unpredictability. Our Borgias, Brutus, and Judas weren't sure he'd accept Sidonise's sharkstew, or even if the latter would be able to reach him. Same concern goes for Doudou-Ménar and her poisoned grapefruit. So, while Sidonise combs the town during the day, Sucette beats the drums at night in order to lure him under the tamarind, and Doudou-Ménar (like the witch giving her apple to Snow White) offers him her deadly fruit. Perchance our man runs into Brutus by the columns and Judas on the Mount of Olives at the same time, he falls into both traps! Sidonise, having already struck, alerts the others. Clamoring with this news to Sucette and Doudou-Ménar, they realize that there too Solibo has swallowed the bait. They then sit down to watch the spectacle of his agony, so fully expected that his fall and scream *Patat' sa!* doesn't surprise a soul. Quietly (Congo having amplified the effect of the untraceable poison), they savor their vengeance to the fullest, which explains why they were still present at the time of your rather surprising arrival, Doudou-Ménar was only supposed to go get a doctor . . . Bouaffesse says: Hmm . . . Sidonise doesn't seem to hate Solibo, and that old Congo took his clothes off to cover the body, he even broke the window with his head when I tried to weigh the cadaver with the tools of science . . . These aren't gestures of hate . . .

The Brain retorts: Sidonise hides her game well, but her strange fainting confirms my hypothesis. I will unmask her at the next questioning. As for Congo, it's all cinematics. Too dramatic, although respect for the dead is exaggerated in the elderly. And let's not forget, he claims to be a maker of manioc graters. Well, the manioc secretes one of the most vicious poisons in the country. Dr. Lélonette is going to extract a strong dose of it from Solibo's liver. Now we're going to question the main suspects: the old quimboiseur and the drum man. Then we'll get the one named Sidonise back in here. They're going to have to spit it all out: the reason for their quarrel with Solibo, the type of poison, the names of their accomplices . . . Tomorrow Lélonette will confirm the poison, and we'll bring the case all wrapped up to the district attorney . . . Bouaffesse, happy with such a wonderful formulation of his poisoning theory, exclaims: You are some brain! . . . Pilon doesn't answer (modesty).

Night was upon them when Congo and Sucette were brought to the bench before the Chief Inspector's desk.

Around 6:30 P.M., once the crowd by the memorial had been dispersed, patrol cars, motorcycles, and inspectors returned to the fold for some administrative formalities, and the police station seemed to wake up. Night recovered its rights as soon as the night shift checked in, sending stairs and halls back into the echoes of oblivion. Amidst such agitation, Pilon had drawn up a new, simpler diagram involving the names of Congo, Sucette, and Sidonise. He had also called the commissioner, the D.A., then without putting down the phone called his chabine to ask her how his children's Carnival went. Making no phone calls, not even to his coolie, Bouaffesse (accompanied by Jambette and Diab-Anba-Feuilles) organized the desk in anticipation of the depositions to come. You'd take them for predators swooping for blood, because, misericordia, the friendly chit-chat Q&A's were over, yes Lord . . .

They manhandle Congo without pity. Jambette and Diab-Anba-Feuilles twist his arms behind his back, slam him onto a chair, face under a desk lamp's incandescence. The old man doesn't defend himself. His eyes, ancient pebbles surfacing in the rivers at Carême, give him an impenetrable air. Bouaffesse has recentered his typewriter, he's sitting on one of the corners of the desk. The Chief Inspector is no more than a shadow behind the lamp. Backs against the door, Jambette and Diab-Anba-Feuilles stretch, impatient, forgetting about Sucette twisted around and cuffed to the bench in the hall. No one says jack. The open window steals no fresh air from the night. Only a few distant cars coming and going are still alive. Under the lamp, the old man's skin shines like varnished West Indian cedar. Soon, sweat inundates him, he says: *Ha hanfê hot,* What'd I do to you? . . . , but no one answers.

. . .

More than fifteen minutes go by. The Chief Inspector
was watching the old man for a hopeless look in his eye, the
pulsing of a vein that signals the shattering of some planned
defense. Picking up nothing, he decided his next course of
action. Mr. Bateau Français, inform us of the nature of the
poison you supplied for Solibo Magnificent's murder . . .
While asking his question, he went through the records
(still on file despite the amnesties) the archivist had ex-
humed for him: Bateau Français, nicknamed Congo, had
been convicted in 1900 for arson, burning a béké's field
during that memorable strike year. In 1935, another historic
strike, he had been kept for a few days following a fist-
warming party at the plantation. Next came a few fines for
thefts of agricultural products and public intoxication, but
he wasn't classified as a quimboiseur or séancier. *Hot ahan
ah hahê houazon,* said Congo, *hantan-an hé an hôjet pahol la
hi hépann Holibo* . . . In front of the faces his superiors were
making, Diab-Anba-Feuilles translated without waiting:
He says that you are looking for poison though it's a strangulation that has culled Solibo . . . Bouaffesse rolled up his
sleeves, Pilon came nearer.

—Did you know Madame Lolita Boidevan?

—*Hi moun,* who?

—Doudou-Ménar . . .

—*Awa,* no!

—Antoinette Maria-Jésus Sidonise, the sherbet vendor?

—*Awa!*

—Eloi Apollon, nicknamed Sucette?

—*Hi là hep mwen . . . iha menyen hanbou . . .*

—He says yes that's the drum man . . .

—Have you run into any of these people lately?

—*Awa!*

Bouaffesse intervened: Papa, listen to me, we respect your white hair, but for us, murderers like you don't have any hair. Looking at you, I see you're the kind of person who has knowledge of the herbs that can poison people faster than yellow snakes . . .

—*Awa!*

The Chief Sergeant seized a huge register he had set aside and brought it down on the old blackman's skull like a plague (the bad kind).

Solibo was of the word, but Congo was of the manioc. Culinary references are also inscribed in our history. Salt pork speaks of the maritime epoch, when boats fed us during the sweats of the first plantations. Then came the colonial period during which the béké tolerated our garden plots. Then we ate yam, dasheen, and grew peas and manioc—*O king manioc!* . . . which weaned us from the breast, with its milk and cream. We ate it as cassava, bread, cake, cookies. It accompanied the peas, powdered the ribs and all the sauces over the scrawny pig. It went well with syrup and gave us starch and flour. Around its goodness bloomed the jobs and tools for its preparation, because before it was harmless you had to grate it, purge it of its venom in snaky sacks of gauze, pass it through the mountain-palm sieves, then dry it in the huge cisterns. After that came the tasks of distribution, sale, transformation. In those days everyone had some of those little home graters Congo made. He hadn't been the only one to sell them in the country, but now he was the last. During his youth, Congo had been a field worker. His unflinching participation in the agricultural strikes made him a pariah. No overseer called his name any longer on hiring day. He had to find himself another way to live. The manioc epoch being favorable to creative spirits, Congo made graters which he sold for a few centimes or bartered for vegetables. He went from house to house, a big sack on his back. His clients called him Congo, his father having been one of those men transported to the country well after slavery. Their African purity had seemed a defect in the middle of our mixed population, and one said "Congo" with as much disdain as "Negro." The Made-in-France stuff undid the manioc, putting it out of our way and even our memory. Now, wheat flour was needed for bread. Eating well meant eating steak & french fries. Congo still continued to make useless graters in his Lamentin hutch. He was the last, once a week, to hawk them obstinately around the markets or in front of bars. His anachronistic silhouette, stooped beneath a guano bag, walking along the shop windows and through traffic, a hopeless symbol of those epochs when we had been different and from which now everyone turned away—and those who looked at him saw our four hundred years.

Congo never missed the Carnival. On that fateful day on which Solibo cashed in his chips, he had walked to Fort-de-France along the highway, without dragging his bag of bewildering graters. It being time to sip punch on his tab at Chez Chinotte, he must have gone to the Savanna to contemplate the floats and the arrival of the vidés. Congo had enjoyed himself: tourists and spectators thought he was disguised. They clapped on seeing him, for no good reason, laughed at him though he didn't try to amuse them, and insisted on taking pictures of him with their children on his knees, or with a woman holding his hand. Sometimes he'd run away from his fans to join a real good vidé, to scream, gesticulate for a few feet, then collapse under a tamarind trying to catch his breath. With the night, he had rejoined the game tables and the rounds of serbi, but the players hated seeing him around, suspecting in his appearance an aptitude for evil deeds: Hey, ol' blackman, get lost, I'm calling out my bet here! . . . Congo walked away, chuckling. Sometimes he remained anchored before the dice, looking real somber. The superstitious player calmed down quick and walked off taking big steps, hand on his quimbois charm. Fatigue descending upon him, Congo was about to return to Lamentin Bay, when the sound of a drum (or of fate) pulled him to the memorial. Under a tamarind, he saw Sucette riding his ka-drum. By his side, Solibo spoke only to the ear of his audience. The old man jumped for joy when he recognized the Master, so rare lately and—this would be his bane—he had joined us to give a hand with the vocals.

They made him undress and kneel on a square, they hammered his skull and ears with thick phonebooks, they kicked him, and made him crawl under office chairs, they knocked him in the liver, the balls, the nape, they crushed his fingers and blinded him with their thumbs. He who had known so much pain and so many miseries discovered a thousand more, punctuated by the Chief Inspector's tranquil and innocent voice asking: Who killed Solibo, Mr. Congo—and how?

When he passed out, they took out their ammonia and brought him back to the pain. When he cried, they laughed. When, having lost his nerve, he laughed, they doubled their ferocity and hammered on. If he was quiet they exerted all their force on him, and when he yelled they gladly gagged him. They wouldn't let him breathe in or breathe out, as if they had put him into one of his own manioc graters and turned turned turned to the rhythm of the Chief Inspector's obsessed voice: What poison did you use, Mr. Congo, well, what poison? . . .

. . .

One word: there was nothing human around there. Congo wasn't admitting anything, and the idea of failing removed any restraint they might have had, so the most primitive part of their brains took over and justified their hate (all night).

Pilon stayed out of the way. The Chief Sergeant directed operations. The desk now looked like a mulatto's field after being trampled by a pack of mounted gendarmes. Congo bounced between Jambette and Diab-Anba-Feuilles. Bouaffesse chipped in like a coach: to emphasize, supplement, do over, augment (all night).

—Now, we have to leave him alone, said Bouaffesse to Pilon, the meat on his bones is going to swell and he'll soon find out what kind a job we did on him . . . Where's the other one?

Eloi Apollon, nicknamed Sucette, received his first slaps in the hall. They lobbed him into the office and caught him between two huge notebooks on the volley. He came to know nine agonies and three knockouts before Pilon questioned him: How did you know Solibo would speak under the tamarind? Did you spend the day with him? . . . Sucette said that the Magnificent never announced anything. Of that fatal evening in the Savanna he had said only last week at the Chez Chinotte: *Sucette, bring your drum under the tamarind tree, on one of the Carnival days* . . . Solibo liked to churn out words during these nights of jubilation, but no one knew when, in what spot and at what length. But during this Carnival, he had disappeared, and his mouth had opened nowhere. I came under the tamarind that night as I had done the night before and the night before that for nothing, the listeners did the same. I could have beaten all the misery out of the ka without seeing the tips of his varnished cowboy boots, to see him come had been the surprise—Pilon got angry: how can one explain the fact that Solibo died at his side without him realizing it? What could this man have done to him for him to foment his poisoning with help from the others? What was the poison used? Congo has already revealed it to us but we want to hear it from you . . . Who did this? Who did that? . . . —then, after the torture, they put him aside so that the meat on his bones could hurt (for the rest of the night).

At dawn, it was useless to hit Congo. Bouaffesse's art radiated all its power from within: the Relic coiled, arched, cried with fright when they feigned coming near him. The Chief Sergeant sneered and said: He is ripe now . . . Diagram in one hand, a glass of coffee in the other, the Chief Inspector was getting his questions in gear, when in a single leap the old man flew right through the window. There was a brief silence before they heard him crash two floors below, louder than a conch smashed by a sailor's cutlass.

The policemen had no time to know what to feel. Congo defenestrated, Sucette let loose his stale horror. Strangely enough, he also attempted a leap toward the void, but Bouaffesse was able to collar him and pin him against the file cabinet. The policemen watched with surprise as Sucette picked it up and threw it at them as easily as a bag of spiderwort. Bouaffesse, Pilon, and Jambette were able to avoid the enormous mass, Diab-Anba-Feuilles alone was swallowed by it like a flat skiff in a tidal wave. He shrieked like a rat in a trap as most of his bones splintered. Sucette, all fury, choke-held Jambette until the latter fainted, then, armed with a club, gave Bouaffesse a magnificent beating (the only one of his life, they say). The Chief Sergeant had almost succumbed, when Pilon took a gun from his drawer and fired into the ceiling. Sucette became pitiful once again; broken by the shot, he flattened out under the desk. Bouaffesse caught him, initiating him to a variety of lynching. In no time, hall and office filled up with policemen in blue or in civilian dress, guns and clubs out, looking for someone to demolish, death knells blinking in their eyes . . .

Sucette is shackled up with cuffs in a strange position. Bouaffesse and a few others pick up the cabinet with great effort. Under it, Diab-Anba-Feuilles is suffocating, his body mushed into a square. Get a doctor, quick! Bouaffesse cries out. Through the window, Pilon observes what's left of Congo. A few curious passersby, coming from dances, are already buzzing about the body. Some patrolmen rush up, disperse them, cover the body, and then mechanically look up. Pilon waves to them, then returns to the desk where Bouaffesse is already acting out a breathtaking escape attempt for the policery with his very own characteristic violence, if-you-pleeze, because you must know that he gave me a jab in the throat, then he tried to leave through the window like he was Spiderman, I tell him: Don't do it, Papa! you're going to fall! Didn't I, Inspestor, we all tell him: Stop that, Papa! But he doesn't listen to anyone, I hold out my hand, he bites it and vaults, flwap! and down he goes like a ripe mango . . . Pilon is no longer listening. He's thinking while he puts things in order: the dossiers, the phone, the big notebooks, Congo's and Sucette's clothes. One of the photos of Solibo's body slips out of the bulging folder. The Chief Inspector looks at it. He's still looking at it when the ambulance comes to take Diab-Anba-Feuilles away and a police car gathers Congo's remains in a plastic bag. For the first time since the beginning of the investigation, Pilon feels ill at ease.

Bouaffesse has lost his good spirits and massages the back of his neck. All the same, he ruminates, that old sorcerer preferred to believe he was the prey rather than admit to the manioc poison. What do we do now? . . . Pilon, mute, puts away the photo and gets up to close the window, reinforcing the heat that bricks up the office. In his handcuffs, Sucette whimpers. The Chief Inspector says: Get this man dressed and put him under tight guard, don't put him with the others, or with Sidonise. I'll write up tonight's report, go home and sleep . . .

—Awa! Inspestor, I stay until the grand finale, Bouaffesse refuses. Jambette, take that dog, put him aside and leave the handcuffs on him, after that go get some sleep, you've done enough today . . .

Bouaffesse has spoken with strength. Inert, the Chief Inspector observes him as if seeing him for the first time. This masculine blackman's incredible authority has dispossessed the Inspector of the inquiry from the start. Pilon even asks himself whether his decisions, his hypotheses, and his actions were really his own. He becomes increasingly ill at ease and presses his eyelids forcefully. Dragging Sucette with him, Jambette complies right away and leaves the room (and the Solibo case).

Evariste Pilon quickly wrote out his report, in which Congo's window suicide became an escape attempt. After that, he gave details of the "mad hysteria" which had overcome Sucette, who had grievously wounded one of the policemen in charge of guarding him. Then he advised the Chief Sergeant to get a doctor's form, as a way of being ready for any eventuality. Finally he asked Dr. Siromiel to come in that morning: it was necessary for the prisoner in custody to get a physical. While Bouaffesse was leaving for the doctor's, Pilon dropped off the report on the commissioner's desk and came back to sit gloomily in front of his notes and diagram—ill at ease.

He was going down the stairs when Bouaffesse reappeared.
—Where're you going?
. . .
—I'm coming!
They took the available unmarked Renault 4L, and injected themselves into Fort-de-France's early morning rush-hour bottleneck. When the traffic got all tied up, they brought out their flashing lights and drove on the sidewalk in a honking inferno. Notebook in hand, crossing out names and addresses one by one, the Chief Inspector carefully checked the suspects' schedules on the day the Magnificent died. The statements checked out: yes so-and-so had come for a drink here, yes so-and-so did this, so-and-so did that, yes Inspekder, so-and-so stayed here until three and then I saw him go down toward the Savanna, correct he ate some cod right here, noo he was alone, she was alone . . . None of the suspects had run into Solibo Magnificent that day. The guests who had been hungry for Sidonise's and Solibo's sharkstew swore that they had watched all the steps of the preparation: the Papa (as they said) hadn't had a portion put aside, and nothing had been added onto his plate, but why're you asking about that, Inspekder? . . . At Doudou-Ménar's, where they announced to Gustave (the ne'er-do-well who takes himself for a Latin because he Spanishes away in a brass band) that his mother (Please accept my distinguished condolences in the name of the Law, said Bouaffesse) was waiting for identification in a drawer at the

morgue, they learned nothing more: No, my mother wasn't anybody's enemy, yes she knew Mr. Solibo but they had never gotten into a fight, she even rather admired him, I think, no, no one named Congo had come here, neither yesterday, nor the day before yesterday, no one named Sucette either. Sidonise? Which Sidonise? . . . When they left Gustave (disconsolado), Pilon studied his diagram, erased a few arrows, crossed out a few names, and told Bouaffesse who understood nothing: It's turning sour . . .

The day has risen in the cell. We were offered sandwiches and coffee. Siromiel examined us from afar and left without a word. We cry. Sidonise and Sucette have disappeared. Congo too. We know that the night has been furious, and we noticed the agitated comings and goings of police and fire-and-rescuemen. From time to time, a guard casts a dumb look through the spyhole. We almost miss Bobé's, Jambette's, and Diab-Anba-Feuilles's possessed eyes . . . Charlo's cheek is ruined by the graveyard leprosy, he prays convulsively. Didon the coolie is sick: he drools, shivers in delirium. Cœurillon cries cries cries, we cry with him. Sometimes I tell them, sobbing: I will recount all this in detail . . . But I get silent faces, the color of papaya and boredom, like the dead souls who served Saint-John Perse, they don't care.

It's noon by the time they reach the small tiled room where Dr. Lélonette performs his autopsies. An assistant standing at his side points the microphone of a recorder toward the expert who announces his observations: distended vessels . . . heart quite larger than a fist . . . very stiff . . . all of this in good condition . . . dark red liver, healthy size . . . dark green bile duct . . . fluid . . . full stomach, contents to be set aside for further . . . While placing this grayish bag in a basin, Dr. Lélonette notices Pilon and Bouaffesse: Ah, here you are! come closer, come closer, come and see these ants ... The cadaver of Solibo Magnificent is covered with them. Almost all of his organs have been taken out, cut into slices, and divided up into different containers. His cranium has been sawed open, the brain extracted. Big blood clots spatter everything, a fetid odor wrestles with that of alcohol and chloroform. Manioc ants swarm over everything, just like under the tamarind. I tried everything to get rid of them, explains Lélonette.

—Where are you at? asks Pilon, who doesn't want to hang around.

Pulling out a kidney, the expert says: I know you're pressed for time, Inspector, but I'll have to have more time, this body is of exceptional quality, see for yourself, there's nothing, nothing (flwap! flwap! he slices the kidney like a ripe mango, and examines the layers one by one and nonchalantly lets them fall in the basin), the man was in perfect health, of exceptional vitality ... What is it, his name, you say? Magnificent? Ah, these people know how to pick their names! ... I completely agree! This body is magnificent ... The problem for me is that he presents all the symptoms of death by strangulation (he opens the wide hole of the neck and takes out a grayish pipe, corrugated, full of thick and reddish bubbles), his larynx, his vocal cords, the whole throat seems to have suffered an extremely traumatic event ... almost to the point of a throat-cutting ... however, on the neck's exterior, yes, yes, look, the neck shows no hematoma, not a trace, it's perfectly normal: this Mr. Solibo would have then had to have been strangled from the *inside* (Whaat? bleat Pilon and Bouaffesse), which literally makes no sense, you'll agree ...

. . .

Indifferent to the policemen's strangled looks, the expert-doctor plunges again into the Magnificent's innards: I looked for poison as you suggested, and I wasted my time . . . I'm waiting on other lab tests, more elaborate, but I think we can put aside that hypothesis at this point . . .

—If he hasn't been poisoned, what method of assasination put him in this state?

—Gentlemen, articulates Lélonette with conviction, this death is mysterious from a medical point of view. As for the police angle, I need a few hours to finish up, but having exhausted all possible external sources of injury, I can already say that there hasn't been a crime. What remains for me to elucidate pertains to the medical realm, strictly medical . . .

—Mothercrocker! Bouaffesse lets out.

—Can I make a phone call? asks Pilon, suddenly feeling weak.

—Go right ahead. The phone is on the wall, you'll get the receptionist . . .

—You're calling about the grapefruit? murmurs Bouaffesse to Pilon, who picks up the phone nervously.

—Yes, it's our last chance . . . Hello, connect me to the Viantot laboratory, please . . . Hello? Dr. Viantot? . . . did you get my little package? the piece of candied fruit . . . yes . . . so? . . . yes, I know, it's grapefruit . . . but what else? . . . nothing? What do you mean, nothing? . . . [1]

---

[1]*Extract from the results given to the Chief Inspector by the laboratory a moment later:* ". . . The sample is, in fact, grapefruit peel cut into slices, definitely scalded and cooked some thirty minutes in water strongly sweetened with brown sugar. We detect, on the surface, some minute traces of grated lemon, nutmeg, and cinnamon. The whole has been covered with sugar glaze. The tests revealed no trace of toxic agents, local or otherwise . . ."

. . .

They drove in silence for about an hour, not knowing where to go. Pilon had sought some kind of salvation from his notes and diagrams. No more coherence. The fine balance of the conspiracy-to-poison had collapsed. Mysteriously, they found themselves back at the tamarind where Solibo Magnificent had touched his horizon. The barricades, still absurdly in place, protected a sinister void: leprous bark, roots in spasm, the remains of night life. Two new guards (whom Bouaffesse dismissed) were walking their melancholy up-and-down. While the guards happily went home, Pilon and Bouaffesse knocked the barricades over, came near the tree which now impaled an ordinary place, without any manioc ants, without the smell of crime, without the aura of conspiracy so supreme the night before. A dusty reality baked the stale urine and dried out the flowers in the sun. The lawmen felt the bark, breathed in the light wind, looking for God knows what. This whole story makes no sense! . . . , Pilon wailed. Bouaffesse didn't answer. A new beard was blurring his cheek, his mustache was as ragged as an old toothbrush. Above and through its shiny and thirsty leaves, the tamarind kept murmuring, and once in a while some knot in its foliage turned into a blackbird. In a few hours, Vaval* would burn with our annual joy, and, among the bumpy roots, Pilon and Bouaffesse seemed already worn out by its approach.

—What do you think "snickt by the word" is? murmured Pilon.

The Chief Sergeant started. Then in a childish guilty voice, he quavered as if at confession: That's exactly what I was asking myself . . . This question exhausted them that morning, because after vain consultations in town Bouaffesse dragged his superior into the back country, toward the deep-depth of the woods, that is to say the furthest away, to a quimboiseur, an expert in strange deaths whom the Chief Sergeant knew and consulted when disappointed with his horoscope. The sorcerer received them in his straw hut of yesteryear inside which the past was frozen in obscure ceramics, calabashes, blackish straw, and in the air saturated with innumerable smells from the hut frame: acacia sap, spoiled locust wood, and the mastic-bully tree's flower-of-eternity. The ancestor no longer had any teeth, his eyes, certainly useless, had let thick eyelids droop over them. Pilon in his confusion found this visit ridiculous, especially since the man looked like Congo. Yet he couldn't repress his avidity when the old man, without even thinking about it, as if he were describing rain, whispered what he knew about snickting by the word. Pilon had it repeated to him one or two times but that didn't get him any further. In the body, Inspekder, the sorcerer revealed in his ageless Creole, there's water and there's breath, speech is breath, breath is strength, strength is the body's idea of life, of its life. Now, Inspekder, stop your thinking, let the dark and the silence weigh in your head, then, as quickly as you can, ask yourself: what happens when life isn't what it should be—and when your mind draws a blank . . . ? —and they concentrated on these questions so hard that they returned from this forgotten ravine with a sack of despair on their minds, Pilon's shoes wouldn't cling to the humid ferns, the sloping spiderwort. The Chief Sergeant found him so unsteady that he held him up by the armpit: there's no use thinking hard when there's no use, Inspestor, no matter what, we couldn't have sent the word to jail! . . . In Evariste Pilon's head the affair ripened, sinuous, vain, derisory, bearing one fruit, one name, one silhouette: Solibo Magnificent. What the suspects had said of that man, words to which he had paid so little attention, was taking shape in his memory just as a new stream begins to act like a river. After asking himself despite the lack of evidence: Who killed Solibo? . . . He was now able to ask the other question: Who, but who was this Solibo, and why "Magnificent"? . . .

During the afternoon, indifferent to the delirium decked in black and white which animated the town, the policemen visited those who had been mentioned as connected with the storyteller. They asked again about improbable enemies but were soon interested only in the man. No one knew his address. Those who spoke more readily or at greater length didn't have a full picture in their heads. Solibo was like a reflection in a window, a sculpture with facets that allowed no angle to reflect the whole. He had existed, people had known him, but only like they know the yellow butterflies which embroider the streets in the breeze just long enough to trace their arabesques in the air. When the night was upon them (Vaval, in flames, reddened the whole harbor), they returned to the police station to release the witnesses—to free us (except for Sucette, found guilty by the judge of willful assault and battery on a law enforcement officer, resisting arrest, etc. . . .), they solicited us again regarding the storyteller's personality. We told them once more the story of Ma Gnam's pig, how Solibo saved her from a mute burial, the circus of the long-one that had hoodooed Ma Goul, the terror that molted the Magnificent's rare enemies into friends. They relearned the essence of the word Solibo, what the second part brought to it, and Sidonise uncovered her heart to them regarding that mystery called love. Then, we left the police station running, plunging the bruises of our pain and fear into the joyful shadows in which Vaval was expiring.

Oh friends, thank you for the favor, the word has been passed on, let's pray that it will last as long as wild sagewood.

Solibo Magnificent was buried in the Trabaut Cemetery under his mother Florise's headstone, in one of those boxes
provided by social services. He went alone, since we were
still hiding in the city's holes, afraid of a new spark in the police inquiry. He would have gone all alone (the police send
nothing to the Obituaries when they clean out their morgue
and social services don't care for ceremony) had the ants,
manioc or otherwise, with or without wings, not landed on
his path and marched with him all day. Upon leaving us,
Sidonise had gone to the morgue, she had banged until
dawn on its whitewashed walls, its blind panes, weighed
down by a dreadful premonition of the coroner's work.
When Lélonette at noon the next day allowed her a visit, she
was zombified, as much by what she saw of Solibo as by, Oh
Lord, what she saw no more. They kicked her out as one
uproots a flower and replanted her in the gardens of the hospital. Her children and Dalta the customs officer came to
pluck her up two months later when the ambulance workers (who always find the time to watch the grass grow) were
moved by the green movement of a breathing vine, of a seeing fruit or stem or leaf.

As soon as I was free, I wanted to forget everything,
even that frivolous promise of writing it all down, of telling
the world about it. Sheltered in my ethnographic work on
the jobbers, I drowned my time writing, wandering with
them between the stalls or behind carts. Running into Pipi
or Didon brought back to my memory and to my heart the
grief I didn't want to face. The sight of the Chief Inspector
shook me from this neurotic stupor to plunge me into yet
another trauma. When I saw him approaching me one market morning, my first impulse was to run away, afraid of being a victim again. But fear paralyzed me, and so he was
able to talk to me in an innocent voice. He told me about his

attempts to limit Sucette's sentence, which were without success since Diab-Anba-Feuilles now limped. He also claimed to have lighted Saint Anthony candles on the graves of Doudou-Ménar and Congo. For about eight months he had been obsessed with Solibo and had pursued an entirely personal (and harmless) inquiry about storytellers and particularly about the one who was for him their archetype. He had found out that the Magnificent had been losing his listeners in his latter days. Solibo wanted to inscribe his words in our ordinary life, but our life no longer had ears nor hollows where an echo could abide eternal. Besides a few out-of-the-way places, the Robert Factory's marina festival, two or three parish feasts, the space for such folklore was dwindling. Organizers of the cultural festival had often solicited him for storytelling bits, but Solibo, dreading these kinds of conservation measures where you left life's theater to stand within an artificial frame, had given mysterious excuses. Only the dumb yam, he used to say, holds out its root for you to yank it out of its home. This transition between his epoch of memory passed down orally, of resistance in the curves of speech, and this new time, when things only survived through writing, just ate him up. His ever-growing piles of charcoal announced his end. He no longer sold anything. Stubborn and desperately cheerful, he brought back bags and bags of charcoal from his oven, which piled up on the other bags, forming pyramids. No one saw the despair in his words, you could barely hear it, the growing void in his words, the burgeoning silence, the shaky lip where fear lodged. He disappeared from the market, but only a few ancestors noticed. Not one client expressed a wish for his return or even questioned his absence, or put aside money for his charcoal, which the town watchman soon took away. We still saw him going by, always walking and walking very quickly, busy as one who fears he won't be so for very long.

Some said he hadn't changed, that he wasn't really quieter than usual. Others affirmed that his speech had dried up, that a void now lived in his voice. People only remembered him when they saw him, and he became dissipated in their memories. He had seen the tales die, Creole lose its strength, he had seen our speech lose that speed that not one of the remaining storytellers ever brought back, he found himself submerged by the reality he had thought he could vanquish. So he spoke to the only one who could understand him, and we saw him go by with his lips beating out silence, talking to himself. There were two of him, but out of tune with each other: abruptly stopping too many times while walking, arms flying in the air too many times, too much hesitation choosing the path at a crossroads. One heard him laughing those laughs which were tragedies. One caught on his face those soulless smiles, eyes opened onto abysses. Oh, he was still elegant and playful, they said, but he was speaking less and less. When you know that in his day he used to light up the sky every night with words, would break into day with them, and that now he would go without an audience for moonful and moonless nights, morning, noon, and evening, all year round, then you can imagine and understand: a stream of words must have been torturing his belly, rolling up in his chest, and waiting for that terrible moment in the Carnival when the hurricane exploded from his throat—devastating. We had to, Pilon concluded, transmit at least the essence of what had been in fact his will . . . He left, oh friends, without me casting a glance or saying a word to him, so tormented was I by this recollection of what I knew, of what we all knew and had always known but in a fragmented way.

What he had been trying to do hit me only a couple knocks later, but abruptly, like the way cayman season comes. Taking hold of me again, the memory of the Magnificent broke all the locks and I was right smack in the whole affair again, from the Master's dazzling words to the cruel police tricks. But write? How to write Solibo's words? In rereading my first notes from the time I followed him around the market, I understood that to write down the word was nothing but betrayal, you lost the intonations, the parody, the storyteller's gestures, and all of this was made even more unthinkable for I knew Solibo was hostile to it. But I called myself a "word scratcher," a pathetic gatherer of elusive things, like the draft through the wind's cathedrals. Pierced with an obscure desire, I devoted my days to carting off water in baskets, sketching silhouettes of dissolving things, elucidating through the market's weave a fresco disappearing in the quicksand of abyss and renewal. I made myself a scratcher of uninscribable words, and I intoxicated myself by riding shadows, so much so that I'd spend weeks recalling what the Master said, searching out his tone, the look in his eyes, the moments when his amused expression belied the gravity of his sentences, and those times when the fear that danced in his eyes only fed the flowers of laughter. I ran into my companions, survivors of that criminal custody, and I tried to reconstitute the storyteller's verbal garland of that night, taking no notes, letting my memory play. For a bushel of seasons (green mango season, the time of watermelon, red snapper time, tuna season) I would find a few of the survivors under the fatal tamarind: each formulated in the Magnificent's way some of the themes he used to embroider upon, the others gave the replies, and Sucette the support of his ka-drum. *Oh friends, the word isn't tame!* . . . Some lacked breath, others rhythm, not one succeeded in wedding the tone to the gesture: at the work of the voice, the body felt heavy, when the gesture took off, the voice disappeared. Pipi, master jobber, taken with a pronounced desire to save the Magnificent's words, tried to perform for more than three hours at the rate of the wooden horses of our Creole merry-go-round. I taped him and then spent the rest of the season *translating* the whole thing onto a whole bunch of whirling and unreadable pages. So then, friends, I decided to squeeze out a reduced, organized, *written* version, a kind of ersatz of what the Master had been that night: it was clear now that his words, his true words, all of his words, were lost for all of us—and forever.

I was so affected that I went to the police station (oh heedlessness!) in order to inform Pilon of that final sorrow, to read him my pathetic writing.[1] I inexplicably needed him to have it, he who hadn't known Solibo in his most handsome days. He met me, accompanied by Bouaffesse. The two of them listened religiously while I mumbled my way through the Magnificent's words, then they got up and took the case file from the cabinet. By the time they had stapled their police and lab reports, the photos that represented nothing, and tied up their fat shit-filled dossier to take it down to the archives (meaning a useless investigation had been closed) they had discovered that this man, who will have only wind and indifferent memories for a resting place, was the suffering pulse of a world coming to an end, and all of their doings had touched just one lonely swell of his last breath.

---

[1] See "After the Word."

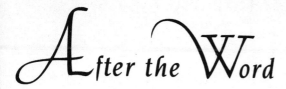

After the Word

Document of the Memory

Sequence of Sucette's Solo

(at the moment that Solibo Magnificent is crossed out)

Plakatak,

Bling, Pitting, Pittingg,

Tak!

Pitak, Blookootoom bootoom

Blookootookootoom Pitak

Tak!

Tak Patak! Kling

Pitting, Pitting, Pittingg

Blookootoom! . . .

When Solibo Spoke

Ladies and gentlemen if I say good evening it's because it isn't day and if I don't say good night it's the cause of which the night will be white tonight like a scrawny pig on his bad day at the market and even whiter than a sunless béké under his take-a-stroll umbrella in the middle of a canefield *é krii?* . . .

é kraa!

but if the béké is in the canefield he always stands on his horse straight and high as a whisk in a canari while in the grass under the cane not above but right under it's the congo* who sweats though he knows no fwrench to say jack for someone to understand and without even understanding a fucking thing that there are countries you know where the sea is in front and behind where the sea is on port and starboard and where the country's greatest path is the sea which doesn't even make a path for a canoe nor two nor seventeen thousand canoes because if there was a path even a tiny bit of path within another tiny bit of path I would have already tramped on it for myself I Solibo who speaks to you here standing as badly on this earth as on one wave two waves three waves et cetera waves and a thousand times more if you want but that don't patter-batter-matter Hortense would say dancing up some intrigue-pretense *misticrii?*

misticraaa!

Hortense dances up some intrigue-pretense but around here not one half a man will dance this evening because the night will be white to listen you gotta wait wait n' figure even if that congo standing in the grass under the cane don't understand the A.B.C.D. and he listened away anyhow to hear and understand lean and glean life with his head's nets since no kind of long-one ever got near his ankles and when he took the Vauclin Mountain path no kinda dog or bulldog with big mean teeth could come near the smoke of his fire because he knew the mountain path without having seen or known her while us blackmen with the A.B.C.D. we sing Vauclin Mountain, don't know Voklin Montin dunno Voklin Montin dunno it no while that congo has lugged his body up the very peak of that mountain and begins to tame a life with no chains no békés no brutes no whips that no plantashun-blackman can join without bringing toughluck, all kinda trouble and multilingo luvyourbrother and at gospel everyone gittup when things flare up for chiggers and mosquitoes *é kriii?*

kraaa!

that kongo dunno his A.B.C.D. and we can laugh but on the mountain he stands at attention only before the sky and the sun while us blackmen with the A.B.C.D. we stand before the gospel before the A before the B before the C before the D yes boss thank you boss and I myself Solibo who can talk in the mouth I yell *Vive de Gaulle* on July 14 even if I draw and quarter my mouth wide to yell *Vive de Gaulle* and I walk in step but I quarter my mouth wide like the sweets vendor who yells cakes cakes cakes she can talk in the mouth to holler holler cakes cakes cakes but her cakes are good and she can speak but I I I Solibo you say that I am magnificent but if I am magnificent what have I got to say and who told me to say it? no one no one told me to say it besides I've got nothing to say I say my say without commander manager boss chief and sergeant fuck the word that don't stand for nothing and oh shit for the blackman whose speech has been given to him, answer me here!

oh shit for that blackman

and if they tell you who gave Solibo words? who gave Solibo words? you say no yes no because if one day someone gives Solibo words all you plantashun blackmen hear me if someone gives Solibo words Solibo has no more words ain't no mo' words?

no, he doesn't have the word!

well who give him the word?

no one gave him the word!

he doesn't have the word and he says that no one gave him the word but Solibo is magnificent because he speaks and you get upset because you want to tell Solibo Solibo steal and bring us some word of the tales about Br'er Tiger, Br'er Rabbit, about the spirits of Ti-Jean and Nanie-Rosette but Solibo shuts his mouth about that and Solibo says that he's no bajoler[1] that he isn't there tonight to give lessons or to make you roll on the ground laughing kia kia kia kia with his turns flip-flap and detours upandaround blo in front frip! slips through the back rat-a-tat? rat-a-ta? who's here? blogodo it's Solibo who doesn't speak tonight through a calabash or through a Tiger that no blackman has ever seen in Tivoli's low woods or in Prêcheur's woods nor in any kind of bushes from around here and what I see here's nothing

---

[1][Solibo's last name is Bajole.]

except some plantashun blackmen not even cunning like Br'er Rabbit who are on this earth as on a dry rock really dry not just a little but really really dry affayou I said affayou?

dia!

knocknock? knocknock? who there? . . . Solibo's the one hollering standing before here in this land who yells planted here on this shaky earth and who says the landscape who says our hill the ravine who tells you to yell the landscape until you thirst for a glass of tafia and to see the real truth and to start hoeing up the truth when I say Fond-Massacre? Fond-Massacre what you say if I say Fond-Massacre? it's not m' sack at the beach but Fond-Massacre where no one knows if it was the long-ones that were massacred there or pigs or rats or any other kind of bloody animal or if it was a group of wretched blackmen the best kind of wretched ones since no one knows who bled here like syrup if it was blackmen or toads so if I say Fond-Massacre, Fond-Massacre answer!

don't know!

was it long-ones or rats?

don't know!

was it some basta'd blackmen or some scrawny pigs?

don't know!

so Solibo says knocknock? it's Soliboscape Solibo from the depths-without-depth Solibo of the forgotten Solibo of the traces without path without Tiger without Rabbit Solibo without sugar without salt natal total hospital congenital bottle municipal jackal clubpodal local grammatical no one's vertical no one's going to make a spectacal knoc-knock? It's the fundamental Solibo, take a deep breath!

fundamental Solibo!

and I stay behind in the country to rummage through the land it's while digging that you find the yam and I stay behind digging the yam in the country even farther until the void fell on me I rummage through the land even in the sweet mother o' nothin' of the day's breadfruits already too sweet and where we drift uselessly on misfortune's boat I rummage through the land and behind the mothers' backs?

I rummage through the land!

and in front of the pink and pale geckos where you eat limestone canaris weeping out little stones?

I rummage through the land!

I rummage through the land with a pitchfork of two languages and a whole field of useless words because around here it's the good-for-nothing who succeeds because when my fog goes away is Mount Pelée hatless?[1]

Morne-Rouge!

and I've got the ash of Le Prêcheur whirling around me whirling without wind and I'm a little gray bell standing at attention like a coconut tree?

----

[1][What follows is a kind of guessing game, the answers to which are various places in Martinique.]

l'Anse-Céron!

and I only have boulevards of cement not streets but boulevards of this and boulevards of that which turn under one or two huge cliffs before the most angry sea?

Grand-Rivière!

and on the hill I throw seventeen thousand stairs which rise rise rise without ever coming down again by the river that Césaire has stopped with lead?

Rive-Droite-Levassor!

and I've got all the earth's and the sky's mosquitoes along with the sardinia-snatches?

Rivière-Salée!

and on my sandy face dripping drool I yell I yell I yell without unlodging a rock that's trying to escape us?

Diamant!

and my water is white?

Saint-Joseph!

and Schœlcher stole my name?

Case-Navire!

and I'm all pain without the cure-all herb where you dance without music you get seventeen slaps without a single hand where you leave the boat to get all bent out of shape in congestion desolation convulsion obsession and extermination how can you say what on earth that is?

we don't know!

Pointe-des-Nègres! my children Pointe-des-Nègres pass me the demijohn you thirsties and Sucette give me a word from the ka about the Pointe

(here, Sucette gave a good dose of ka)

because the Pointe my children is the beginning of the first the beforall without turning back to go round go up come back down and you gotta pull the Poynt all of the Pointe to coffitup suckitup no use crying nia nia nia but to work the land and live there by cunning man hutch or like the last bottle in the country of thirsty throats to wrap around the primordial and the initial the first with the next and plan around here on the native soil like what native-natal?

like fundamental Solibo!

oh mourn my children mourn Gogo the bird which thought it good to drown because his throat was a bit dry by where again?

right here!

good my children Doudou-Ménar let me taste your candied fruits so that some sweet syrup might come down behind my throat which is larger than the nose-hole of a suffocated man roll in my stomach and light my insides like the shepherd star lights a piece of the sky at the hour when men drink a good glass of rum for Jesus and say like the priest?

amen!

get the demijohn get the ants get the sky the earth and the seventeen curses which bring upon the country some kind of volcanic eruption and judge oh my children if Solibo shouldn't see the end of the Carnival tell Vaval that in his arthritic third left toe the pain comes from Solibo who cries nia nia nia like the Gueydon Fountain when ten thousand rains have lowered the hills and then all kinds of filth rotten wood and garbage come down and who cries not over life because life around here isn't worth a stale stuffed land crab but who cries to scour the coconut white of his eyes to scour the sidewalks to scour his eye sockets and who wants to go home to the other side and inside himself with brand new eyes full of the light of the Wonder battery which don't get used up like wunderbatteries

UNLESS YOU USE IT!

if one was to cry over life here which isn't worth a canari of rotten meat I would have cried the syrup that Antoinise gave off under my touch, right after the start of my touch under the light-light delicate touch Antoinise let her syrup drip between my fingers, a DO syrup, a RE syrup, a DO RE MI FA SOL syrup doe a deer . . . ah DO RE MI FA SOL LA TI, Christ don't you know that song?

DO—DO LA TI DO!

and if one ask why then is Solibo crying nia nia nia when it's time to go say that he's weeping over Antoinise's syrup, her dear drops of syrup, sweeter than the first sweet thing that a hungry man sucks after a thousand bites on a chunk of salted meat when no fountain flows for him and when no one gives him a glass of water DO DOE a deer

DOO—DO LA TI DO!

so kids if you see Solibo dead and Gwadloup comes to furrow his body bury him under a barrel of rum no crying kids 'cause under the barrel Solibo will be partying every drop of rum of the barrel of rum will flow down his throat for rum bury him under the barrel kids bury him under the barrel and when the priest comes give him rum for his sprinkler Solibo will be happy every drop of rum from the rum sprinkler will flow down his rum snout and if the priest says *et spiritus sanctus* will you reply with the song?

SECULARUM IS RUM!

if the priest says *dominus vobiscum?*

SECULARUM IS RUM!

and under the barrel Solibo will be all joy he'll go to the countryless land where the sky is thirteen colors plus the last color where all the weeds grow less often than the pacala yams where Air-France got no terminal and where the békés ain't got no kind of plantation factory or big store where the charcoal needs no fire and where the fire rises without charcoal where you see children flying with wasps and butterflies where the sun is a big ka-drum and the moon is a lute where the blackman is all joy all music all dance all syrup on life's back and where oh children where Solibo himself despite his big mouth and his big tongue and his big throat will no longer need ... hugckh ... PATAT' SA! ...

PATAT' SI! ...

Bringing the Word

$\mathscr{A}$fterword

Sublime Tumble
by Rose-Myriam Réjouis

Is it right that a man should abandon his mother tongue for someone else's? It looks like a dreadful betrayal and produces a guilty feeling. But for me there is no other choice. I have been given the language and I intend to use it.

CHINUA ACHEBE

This book, *Decolonizing the Mind,* is my farewell to English as a vehicle for any of my writings. From now on it is Gikuyu and Kiswahili all the way.

NGUGI WA THIONGO

There is the buried language and there is the individual vocabulary. . . . Tonally the individual voice is a dialect; it shapes its own accents, its own vocabulary and melody in defiance of an imperial concept of language, the language of Ozymandias, libraries and dictionaries, law courts and critics, and churches and universities, political dogma, the diction of institutions. . . . Deprived of their original language, the captured and indentured tribes create their own, accreting and secreting fragments of an old, an epic vocabulary, from Asia and from Africa, but to an ancestral, an ecstatic rhythm in the blood that cannot be subdued by slavery or indenture, while nouns are renamed and the given names of places accepted like Felicity village or Choiseul. The original language dissolves from the exhaustion of distance like fog trying to cross an ocean, but this process of renaming, of finding new metaphors, is the same process that the poet faces every morning of his working day, making his own tools like Crusoe, assembling nouns from necessity, from Felicity, even renaming himself. That is the basis of the Antillean experience, this shipwreck of fragments, these echoes, these shards of a huge tribal vocabulary, these partially remembered customs, and they are not decayed but strong.

DEREK WALCOTT

"Neither Europeans, nor Africans, nor Asians, we proclaim ourselves Creoles" is the first sentence of *Eloge de la Créolité,* a manifesto written by Jean Bernabé, Patrick Chamoiseau, and Raphael Confiant. Inspired by Edouard Glissant's *Discours Antillais,* Créolité is a "'literary project' designed to keep the Creole language alive," a reaction against alienation. In *Solibo Magnificent* (1988), individual artistic creativity comes to the service of this cultural and linguistic movement of self-discovery and assertion. And while language issues have become a kind of Bermuda Triangle for many postcolonial writers and critics, Chamoiseau succeeds in further enriching his text by making its plot, narrative structure, themes, revolve around and evolve from the complex internal, sociolinguistic reality of Martinique.

To begin with, Solibo Magnificent, the novel's central figure, dies, on the first page, "throat snickt by the word," the spoken word (*égorgette de la parole*). Such a death is surreal both because *égorgette* is Chamoiseau's neologism and because, to echo the skeptics in the novel, "one does not die that way." Throughout the novel, the magical reality of his death speaks of the allegorical critical condition of a Creole oral culture likewise dying of an *égorgette de la parole.* It is the realization of having outlived his time, the era of oral Creole expression, that prompts the storyteller's literary death, his retreat before a world in which there is less and less room for orality. But as Solibo goes limp (and then stiff) before the reader's eyes, Chamoiseau, his prodigal yet illegimate (the Creole *yich dewô,* "outside child," may be more appropriate) son-in-spirit, begins to wrestle with language and with the written word. The old storyteller makes way for a new kind of story writing: the final page of his life is also the first page of "Ti-Zibié's" novel.

In choosing writing over speaking, Chamoiseau opts for artistic survival—he will not go the way of Solibo. But if Chamoiseau calls himself a "word scratcher," a self-deprecating and self-conscious narrator, it is perhaps because he has knowingly made this choice despite Solibo's warnings:

> One writes but words, not the word, you should have spoken. To write is to take the conch out of the sea to shout: here's the conch! The word replies: where's the sea? But that's not the most important thing. I'm going and you're staying. I spoke but you, you're writing, announcing that you come from the word. You give me your hand over the distance. It's all very nice, but you just touch the distance ... Stop scribbling scritch-scratch, and listen: to stiffen, to break the rhythm, is to call on death ... Ti-Zibié, your pen will make you die, you poor bastard ...

Mistrusting the singularity of a deaf, monotone narration, as well as the arrogance and lie of the literary omniscience of the Western novel, Ti-Zibié, at the impromptu wake held in honor of the departed, co-narrates the literary eulogy along with the echo of Solibo's words and with his faithful audience; and the wordsman comes alive through the transcribed collective accounts. In this way, Solibo's silence turns all of his listeners into storytellers, the tellers of his story. Integrating literary and oral devices, the novel explores the emergence of this plurality of voices. Presenting their tales within a greater tale, Chamoiseau *writes* down the tales and "*tells*" his novel.

Yet, while on the one hand Chamoiseau's text does achieve an artful symbiosis between orality and literature (*oraliture,* as he would call it), it also serves as a sociolinguistic battlefield in its depiction of the burlesque police investigation of the wordsman's death. A polished police text such as Inspector Pilon's report exemplifies the narrative rigidity of the linguistic and cultural frame Chamoiseau wishes to avoid. Erupting into a reality as yet out of its reach, the police translate Solibo's death into a murder and his listeners into suspects, misnaming everything and ravaging lives in order to create a "case" (a work of fiction).

These guardians of the peace constantly wage war against their humbler compatriots. Proud of being on the right side of things, that is, on the right side of the Law ("Made-in-France"), the cops are intolerant, disrespectful, and cruel to those unable to speak French—the language which usually at least ensures a "real" job (generally state employment)—and rise above their "*nègre*" condition. Pitting French against Creole, in order to affirm the authority of the police report—written in elevated French—the police cram and reduce the suspects' Creole reality into the neat blanks (full legal name, permanent address, occupation) of official forms. The cops' manifold use of French underscores both their reverence for that precious resource and a deep-rooted self-loathing. Chief Sergeant Bouaffesse uses it as a sedative to calm his men, as an antidote for Creole passion in a memorable scene which we will come back to, a magic incantation by which he pulls "truth" out of people ("The best way to corner this vicious old blackman was to track him down with French [since it] makes their heads swim, grips their guts, and then they skid like drunks down the pavement"), as a way of reasserting his rank after having translated Congo's Creole into French for Pilon, and as a weapon (holstered in a dictionary) which he uses to shake answers from his victims.

Chief Inspector Pilon, introduced as the brains of the pack, is a bitter pièce de résistance in Chamoiseau's portrayal of the tensions between Creole and French. Though he declares Creole a language, paying lip service to a popular intellectual view, Pilon never speaks it—only French confers status. French is the language in which he obtained all of his diplomas, the language in which he is truly *Inspecteur Pilon*, and it is his tool, his slide rule. It is that mathematical language with which he solves his mysteries and writes his reports. Furthermore, though his speaking French to Creolophone suspects erodes communication throughout this inquiry, Pilon's Cartesian logic never tells him to speak Creole to them, refusing to bathe his tongue in what Bouaffesse calls "the patois of these bums."

Creole, however, which Bouaffesse feels he must translate for Pilon so as not to see a black man who has worked so hard to rise above his condition have to step back into that "mud," is for many the language of the hills, used to express the lower human emotions. Bouaffesse's "mothercrockers!" are always in Creole, and it is also in an "irrepressible Creole" that his deputy Diab-Anba-Feuilles angrily insults the vendor Doudou-Ménar, one of their suspects, when she steps out of line. And it is only at the sound of his French full legal name and of words spoken in a French-French ("Monsieur Figaro Paul, if-you-pleeze, you are forgetting yourself!") that the devil in Diab retreats.

As the administrative and official language, French steadily erects social, economic, and linguistic barriers within Antillean society, forcing out of it those who do not speak the béké's tongue. Spilling out of the police forms that are unsuited for it, Creole reality is labeled illegitimate. And since, for example, there is no French equivalent for "manioc grater maker," the police decide that such a job description cannot be an occupation. French is the language of the educated, of those with first and last names and middle initials, of those who hold real jobs.

In his portrayal of the coexistence of French and Creole in Martinican reality, Chamoiseau also presents the reader with different levels of translation. The example below illustrates not a translation between two languages but really a translation of discourse, of ways of talking:

> Mr. Longue-Bête, what is your age, profession, and permanent address?
> —Huh?
> —The Inspector asks you what hurricane you were born after, what you do for the béké, and what side of town you sleep at night? Bouaffesse specifies.

Here, Bouaffesse translates a question the Chief Inspector asks one of the witnesses, but the translation occurs not from French into Creole—both Bouaffesse and Pilon are speaking French—but from one culture, one class to another.

Chamoiseau should be commended for his rich and poignant portrayal of a Martinican reality in its French-dominated sociolinguistic order, while at the same time embracing a theme so dear to Creole tradition, that of the storyteller. He presents the tensions between the French and Creole languages, cultures, and epistemes, while his text reflects points at which Martinique becomes an intersection of the two. All proponents of Créolité (Martinican or otherwise) should applaud his celebration of the Martinican word and syntax. For despite his use of French, it is Martinique (and to a certain extent, the Caribbean) that is the real presence in this text—France, Africa, and Asia permeate this novel in the way they have and do life in Martinique today.

Despite its generous use of Creole, *Solibo* is not a Creole novel per se, however, a fact that perhaps reveals the true "protagonist" here: Chamoiseau's language. This language is sandwiched between the police report that precedes it ("Before the Word") and an "ersatz" of Solibo's words ("When Solibo Spoke") which along with a "recording" of Sucette's drum solo forms the last section, called "After the Word": the four chapters in the middle—the body of the novel as narrated through an authorial persona—are implicitly designated as "the word" (*la parole*). Both the report, also referred to as the document of the calamity (*l'écrit du malheur*), and Solibo's words, also referred to as the document of memory (*l'écrit du souvenir*), are in a sense Chamoiseau's props, acting as foils to each other while stretching out and framing his canvas. The idea of *la parole* referring to the bulk of the novel is quite evocative, for Chamoiseau is using the word in its French ("language"), Creole ("tale"), and biblical (synonymous with creation, revelation, and God) senses. Chamoiseau's text is thus a tale about the birth of his own linguistic creativity.

Given that he plunges his text into the heart of the aforementioned linguistic Bermuda Triangle at the prow of his *S.S. Créolité,* a superficial assessment of his project in *Solibo* could suggest that he is preoccupied with sorting out issues of diglossia at the price of his art. That is, his stakes, his agenda, are so suicidally high that one is certain he'll come out with nothing. Yet Chamoiseau surfaces with words and a text all his own: *la parole.* Maybe Chamoiseau does not get swept off his feet precisely because he cares not about languages but about Language—in Derek Walcott's sense of poetic language, where each poet must begin "every morning of his working day . . . making his own tools like Crusoe, assembling nouns from necessity, from Felicity, even renaming himself." Nevertheless, the author-narrator-protagonist's explicit obsession with languages and culture somewhat absolves him from ever formulating a clear opinion about them and, thus, of ever taking any clear-cut action, political or otherwise. His preoccupation with Language, the realm of the artist, shields him from plummeting into a politicized and artistically paralyzing obsession with languages.

Chamoiseau makes a paradigm out of the double meaning of the word *Creole,* in order to be both a Martinican writer with an agenda (keeping Creole alive) and an artist in his own right and with his own impulses. On one hand, Creole refers to a concrete people (whom he wants to represent), and on the other, to the vague process of mixing and pastiche (a concept which legitimizes the methods of his art). This renders possible a double reading of his text. The plurality of the narrative voices in his work can be seen both as a written extension of Creole traditions of storytelling and as mere shadow puppetry through which speaks one author-narrator-protagonist. The fact, however, that his novel is not written in Creole but in Chamoiseau-ese cannot detract from its Créolité, as it inherently benefits from the second sense of the term. After all, Creole was born of piracy—literally, French buccaneering, out of the Norman French matrix of Caribbean sailors of old.

Chamoiseau makes no attempt to conceal his uneven knowledge of the cultures between which he is playing. Though he circles around the dynamics and tensions between French and Creole, as one would expect from any good proponent of Créolité, he outruns each and writes in an invented tongue that no one actually speaks, a *Fréole*—to use the neologism Pierre Pinalie employs to describe the semantic strategies in Chamoiseau's earlier novel *Chronique des sept misères*. In choosing neither French nor Creole, Chamoiseau in a sense secedes from both Martinique and France, parallel to the manner in which the Créolité he advocates must break from Africa, Europe, and Asia. In his text, he shakes off the chains of countries and literary movements, since if he wanted to give his all to Créolité he would have also had to write in Creole. Chamoiseau, however, accepts a place in Creole *pre*-literature in order to speak in his own voice. Creole literature is still growing out its fingers, as most Antillean writers are not yet prepared or able to write entirely in this nascent literary tongue. Chamoiseau's *Fréole* is also symbolic of his linguistic, psychological, and cultural situation as a French-educated Creolophone who writes in a language that most of his "compatriots"—be they French or Martinican—do not speak. Chamoiseau speaks neither Creole nor French; he gets his *characters* to do so *for him,* gets *them* to carry the baggage that using standard French or Martinican Creole entails. And at the risk of having his text defaced by readers' misunderstanding, he finds his very own voice and tells his tale—that of the survival of *his* creativity and integrity.

. . .

Chamoiseau's writing is not an orientalism because he does not use Creole as an ornament. It is not exotic; rather, it is idiosyncratic. He cuts, irons, crumples, twists words to fit the order he wants to depict. Though Chamoiseau creates his language, he does not invent words from scratch. For his insistence on being called a word scratcher speaks of his desire to create a palimpsest, to write upon other texts. In this novel, he writes upon Solibo's text, among others. Likewise, this translation writes upon Chamoiseau's text, while using many others, and is thus too a palimpsest. The author-narrator's refusal to be called a writer (as opposed to a word scratcher) reposes greatly on this trope. Chamoiseau chooses a creativity tied to history over one that stresses complete originality, presuming itself as the point of origin. The difference Chamoiseau makes between a writer and a word scratcher can be said to be of the same order as that between interpreting and translating. In both cases, the latter project seems to connote more modesty; though Chamoiseau's text is of course far more than a transcription of oral tales, and translation is indeed interpretation par excellence.

AMHERST, 1994
PRINCETON, 1996

Glosses on Names and Nicknames

Bête-Longue   long-one, snake

Bateau Français   French boat

Boidevan   caution, trouble ahead

Bouaffesse   from *bois-fesse,* stick-for-the-ass or wood-ass

Diab-Anba-Feuilles   devil-in-the-bush

Doudou   sweetheart, darlin'

Evariste   from *avariste,* the Creole word for opportunist

Gros-Liberté: great freedom

Jambette   knife

La Fièvre   fever

Laguinée   literally, Guinea (Africa); in the Americas, a maroon stronghold

Oiseau (as in **Cham-oiseau)**   bird

Oiseau de Cham   another wordplay with author's name, Chamoiseau. *Cham* is the biblical Shem, but when pronounced in Creole as the French *champs* it signifies "fields"; so Oiseau de Cham also connotes "bird of the fields."

Pilon   pestle

Richard Cœurillon   Richard Lionheart

Siromiel   honey

Soleil   sun

Solibo   fall, somersault, pirouette

Sucette   lollipop

Ti-Cal   li'l piece

Ti-Coca   li'l Coke (bottle)

Ti-Zibié   small game

Zaboca   avocado

Glossary

alizé French word for the Antilles trade winds

Antilles used to designate the French West Indies exclusively, in Guadeloupe, in Martinique, and in this novel

bakoua a handmade straw hat of varying size and shape

békés white Creoles of Martinique, members of the old planter class and their descendants

canari (Carib word) an earthenware cooking pot

Carême (French word for Lent) used in the French Antilles to indicate the dry season which lasts from November to June. The wet season from July through October is called *hivernage.*

chabin (masc.), **chabine** (fem.) a light-skinned mixed-race individual with blond or reddish hair and black facial features. European name for a kind of sheep produced by crossbreeding a ewe with a billygoat.

coolie a Martinican East Indian, usually pejorative

congo an African field worker brought to Martinique after the end of slavery; also the descendants of such field workers, usually pejorative

département a French provincial administrative unit. Martinique is a *département,* just as Hawaii is a state; though French *départements* have about as much autonomy as, for example, Puerto Rico. *Départements* are divided into local units called *communes;* Martinique has 34 *communes.*

docoune a Guadeloupean sweet doughnut

dorlis a frightening nocturnal figure who rapes women and carries on conversations with rats

é krii?/é kraa! see **misticrii?/misticraa!** below

féroces a spicy avocado and codfish dish or dip

ka, ka-drum a large traditional drum played with the hands

kalior (Creole slang) a seducer

kilibibi a candy made from sugar, powdered cocoa, corn, and/or nuts

léwoz a dynamic ka-drum rhythm; one of the seven ka rhythms particular to Guadeloupe

macadam a dish made with highly spiced cod, court-bouillon, and rice

madou lemonade or orangeade made with cane syrup (*jus de batterie*)

manger-coulis (literally, coolie food) wild parasitic plants

manioc (also called cassava) a shrubby tropical American plant (*Manihot esculenta*) widely grown for its large, tuberous, starchy roots; the root of this plant, eaten as a staple food in the tropics only after leaching and drying to remove cyanide. Its starch is also the source of tapioca (*American Heritage Dictionary,* Standard Edition). Grated the wrong way, manioc can be poisonous.

matadora (*matadò* in Creole) a woman who triumphs, who wins approval like a matador in the arena. Current usage: a strong, respected, authoritative woman. "Matadora" is our rendering of Chamoiseau's French invention *femme-matador*.

misticrii?/misticraa! a traditional exchange between a storyteller and his audience. The storyteller wants to know whether his listeners are awake . . .

morne the term used throughout the French West Indies to designate the hills of volcanic origin that dot the landscape. Where it is not part of a place name (i.e., Morne-Rouge), we've translated this word as such.

quimboiseur a word describing a magic user, derived from the old tradition of curing known as Quin/Tiens Bois. Quimboiseurs dispense ancient remedies and amulets (*quimbois*); they are professional ritual consultants; also, pejoratively: evildoers.

Savanna a large park in the center of Fort-de-France called "La Savane"

Schœlcher, Victor champion of Martinican abolitionism

serbi a local dice game

soucougnan in West Indian folklore, a creature capable of shedding its human skin at night, flying batlike, and emitting light

Syrians a general term for Martinican Arabs, most of whom are actually Lebanese

tafia white rum

Texaco   a shantytown suburb of Fort-de-France turned *quartier*

Vaval   King of Carnival, an effigy symbolizing Carnival, ceremonially burned on Ash Wednesday

vidé   (from the expression "videz les lieux") in the French Antilles, a wild and noisy parade of singers and dancers during Carnival. They are equivalent to mummers: see author's footnote above on page 72.

z'habitant soup   (*soupe z'habitant*), a thick broth made from local vegetables

zouk   Martinican music and dance; also, a general term for a party

Translators' Acknowledgments

The help and encouragement of many people went into the completion of this project. We would like to express our heartfelt appreciation to our families, Anne Halley, Jules Chametzky, Leah Hewitt, Andy Parker, Rhonda Cobham, Michael Kasper, Lucien Taylor, Jim Maraniss, Hershel Farbman, Fred d'Aguiar, Carol Szymanski, Cass Garner, Charlotte Cooney, David Baker, Altie Karper, Susan Fensten, Jeanne Morton, Joan Benham, and Erroll McDonald.

R.M.R.
V.V.

ALSO BY PATRICK CHAMOISEAU

TEXACO

Translated by Rose-Myriam Réjouis and Val Vinokurov

With this passionate, funny, and ceaselessly inventive novel, Patrick Chamoiseau produces nothing less than a mythic history of the Creole nation that arose from the forced marriage of French and African peoples in his native Martinique. The chief spokeswoman for that nation is the indomitable and profanely wise Marie-Sophie Laborieux, the founder of Texaco, a teeming shantytown poised on the edge of a city that constantly threatens to engulf it.

"A great book has been written . . . one with [a] melodic voice and amplitude of heart."
—*The New York Review of Books*

A New York Times *Notable Book*
Fiction/Literature/0-679-75175-0

VINTAGE INTERNATIONAL
Available at your local bookstore, or call toll-free to order:
1-800-793-2665 (credit cards only).